ORANGEFIELD

Al Sarrantonio

ORANGEFIELD

A Novel of Halloween

Other horror titles by Al Sarrantonio:

ORANGEFIELD
A Novel of Halloween

Al Sarrantonio

CEMETERY DANCE PUBLICATIONS

Baltimore

❖ 2002 ❖

To
Ray Bradbury:

Maestro of Halloween

Foreword

The original name of the town was Orangefield, after a Scottish Earl who was little remembered and therefore expendable. But the locals, by referendum in 1930, changed it to Pumpkinfield in order to make money.

"Hell, it *sounds* like Halloween!" was the general consensus. It was hoped that with a name like Pumpkinfield folks would come by and, if disappointed at the lack of pumpkins, would at least enjoy the foliage and spend dollars.

The second choice was Little Salem.

They didn't grow many pumpkins in the region in 1930, but in a bizarre case of the cart leading the horse and then winning the race, it turned out that the soil was richly perfect and that pumpkins grew in profusion — up hillsides, in the fertile valleys, in straight tended rows, in backyard patches. By the late 1930s the place literally turned orange in late summer, and stayed that way until October 31st.

After that, with so many rotting (and smashed) pumpkins, the town smelled sickly sweet for a week.

Just before World War II, another referendum changed the name back to Orangefield.

It was sometime during this period that strange things began to happen in Orangefield — usually around the time of Halloween. There was the disappearance of the entire Cutler family in 1940, leaving behind warm tea and a game of Monopoly in progress. Just after the war there was the murder of Amos Stone by his three children, wearing Halloween masks, aged seven, five, and four, who then went on to murder one another, leaving a knife-induced bloodbath. In 1951 there was the brand-new Sullivan house which went up in flames on its first All Hallows Eve, was rebuilt, and burned down again the following Halloween. And then *again*. (The plot was left fallow after that.) These and other similar stories are covered in the first two volumes of this history. More recently, there was the case of children's book author Peter Kerlan and his wife, who were both killed by hornets in their own house — it was rumored that Kerlan himself had dealings with Samhain, or 'Sam,' as he is known locally. Kerlan's children book *Sam Hain and the Halloween that Almost Wasn't* was published posthumously. The bee-keeper who had alleged this and claimed to have seen Kerlan's death with his own eyes was found hanged in his own backyard two years after Kerlan's death, the rope cinched around a strong oak tree branch next to a hornets nest. Hornets were found crawling in his empty eye sockets. The same year, oddly, the district attorney who had handled Kerlan's death died of a toxic reaction to hornet stings.

There were, and continue to be, many tales of Samhain, the Celtic Lord of Death and master of Halloween, and many so-called 'Sam Sightings.' It has been said that Samhain somehow owns Orangefield, had claimed it before man of any kind — native American or Englishman — had laid plough to the land. There occurred, during the writing of this history, the case of Hattie Ivers, and Corrie Phaeder, the young man who returned to Orangefield and claimed direct confrontation with Samhain himself.

And then there was perhaps the worst thing that ever happened there, which concerned in part my own father...

— Thomas Robert Reynolds, Jr.
Occult Practises in Orangefield and Chicawa County,
New York, Volume Three

PART ONE

Autumn

Chapter One

Call me Sam.

Kathy Marks heard the voice like a cold finger drawn down the inside of her skull. It didn't sound like a voice at all. And it seemed to tickle at the darkest reaches of her memory...

She looked up from the front desk of the Orangefield Library and glanced at the nearest window, which was half covered in a paper pumpkin cutout, crayon-colored side facing outward. Even though the holiday was weeks away, they'd had the annual Halloween drawing contest for the four to eight-year-olds that afternoon, which had culminated in a frenzy of scissor snipping followed by the scotch tape mounting of the winners in the front windows.

There was no one at the window — only the faintest whisper of a chill wind outside, brushing the pane and making it moan.

Idly, Kathy scratched her left arm, gently soothing the ghostly itch of an old scar.

As if on cue, the street lights outside the library winked on, turning autumn twilight bright again. Kathy Marks jumped involuntarily, then laughed lightly, shaking her head.

She turned back to the paperwork on her desk.

The library was closed; the front door had been locked for twenty minutes. Her assistants Marjorie and Paul, high school students earning extra credit, had gone home. Soon she would follow to her own home, such as it was.

There was no hurry.

There never was: she was thirty-two years old and alone. Almost a cliche, the spinster librarian. She had always had the feeling, ever since she was young, that she was waiting for something.

Waiting...

Librarian. Open the door.

There it was again — a wind that sounded like a voice.

This time Kathy looked at the offending window with the same stern stare she used on talkers in the library.

"Don't do it," that stare said, "because I said so."

There was what sounded like a faint chuckle from the window, which then faded to silence.

Something very vague pinged at the back of Kathy's mind, something long ago...

But then it swirled and settled and was gone.

Kathy finished her paperwork, retrieved her handbag and coat, and walked to the front door.

As always, before turning out the lights, she gave a final prim sweep with her gaze across the stacks on the first floor, up the spiral stairs to the second floor balcony, noting with satisfaction the neat short rows of shelves jutting out from the wall, empty retrieval carts in the hallway which ran along the balcony —

No, not empty — one cart was still partly full on the balcony. She would have to talk to Marjorie on Thursday. The girl was obviously in a hormone dither, always flirting instead of doing the few things she had to do —

Something moved behind the cart.

"Who is that?" Kathy Marks snapped immediately. "Who's up there? Come out this minute!"

The cart was still as stone, and there was no sound.

And then, behind her, a dry cold sound at the window again:

Let me in...

Kathy jumped, spun around and faced the nearest window.

A gust of wind rattled the pane.

There was no one there.

She spun on her heel and caught slight movement up on the balcony behind the cart.

"Stand up immediately!" she shouted, angry with herself that her voice sounded a bit hysterical.

As much to get away from the window as anything, she marched to the spiral staircase and mounted it, her footfalls echoing metallically as she circled higher.

She heard a scuttling sound above her, and the front window below rattled again:

Call me Sammy...

Something tugged harder at her memory, and sent a chill through her. Once again, without thinking, she brushed her left forearm with her fingers.

Thoroughly rattled now, Kathy huffed in frustration and fear as she reached the landing. It gave her a view down the balconied corridor to the far wall.

There was no one behind the cart.

Sam...

"Stop that!" she yelled — and at the same moment saw the briefest hint of movement in the short corridor behind the cart, between two shelves.

In a second she was in front of the opening, staring in—

"What—"

A young girl squatting on the floor held up a book protectively in front of her face, as if to ward off a blow. A backpack was beside her on the floor.

"Please don't be mad at me, Ms. Marks! I got here late, and left my library card at home, and—"

"Annabeth Turner?" the librarian replied in disbelief. She stepped forward and yanked the book out of the crouching girl's hands. The exposed face behind it was suffused with a look of remorse and terror and something else — almost defiance.

"Please don't tell my mother! Please just let me go!"

Startled by the girl's frantic reaction, Kathy softened her tone. "Just what were you doing in here? Don't you realize you would have been locked in the library overnight?" She added, in a slightly sterner voice, "Stand up this minute."

The girl did as she was told.

She looked older than her twelve years — thin, pale, almost as tall as the librarian herself, with straight brown hair cut in bangs. Her haircut, her awkwardness, her height, her way of dressing — in obvious hand-me-downs a decade at least out-of-date — made her, even to Kathy Marks's less-than-trendy, Talbot's-styled sensibility, a walking poster girl for peer ridicule.

Something more easily accessed in the librarian, an echo of her own awkward and unhappy past, sympathized with the young girl. When she spoke again her tone was almost gentle.

"Tell me why you tried to stay here overnight, Annabeth."

The girl stared at the floor.

"Trouble at home?" Kathy asked. "I know you haven't lived here long, but believe me, there are people in Orangefield who can help you with—"

"Nothing like that," the girl replied quickly, not looking up, which told the librarian that there may be something there after all.

"Annabeth, look at me."

The young girl raised her head slowly — and Kathy blinked, startled by the intensity in her eyes. She had expected them to be full of tears, but there was that hard, defiant look again.

Recovering, Kathy said, "Is there anything you want to talk to me about? You've spent almost every day since you moved here in July here in the library — first there was the astronomy section you tore through, and then the encyclopedias, and now heaven knows what else. I thought from the talks we've had that maybe we'd become friends. I know how hard it's been on you since your father died, Annabeth. You know I lost my own parents when I was your age—"

"My name is Wizard," the girl announced, "not Annabeth. I don't let anyone call me that anymore."

At a loss for words, the librarian replied, "You still haven't told me why you tried to lock yourself in here—"

"There are books you won't let me take out."

Something that had been lurking at the very back of Kathy Marks's awareness now came forward. She realized they were standing in front of the section marked LOCAL HISTORY.

"You have a project to do on Orangefield? I'm sure I could arrange—"

Her eyes still defiant, the girl answered, "Not that."

Kathy turned over the book she had taken from the girl's hand; the title read *Occult History of Orangefield* by D.A. Withers. There was a RESTRICTED stamp on the cover.

The librarian looked at the girl. "You're interested in ghosts and such?"

An almost secret smile came to the girl's lips. "You could say."

For the first time since the strange interview had started, it occurred to Kathy Marks that the girl standing before her might be on drugs, or worse.

"I want you to give me your home phone number, so I can talk to your mother," the librarian said in a sterner voice than she had yet used. She dug into her bag for the pen and notepad always there.

The girl said nothing, then recited the number in a curt voice.

There was a sudden loud sound below, from the first floor.

The front window with the pumpkins on it began to rattle, as if someone were rapidly knocking on it with a knuckled fist.

The librarian stared at the window, trying to see if anyone was there, but the sound abruptly stopped.

When she turned back to Annabeth the girl had reached down to pick up her backpack.

"I have to go,"Annabeth said. Her voice had become almost sweet, making the librarian reassess her yet again. *The awkward girl, lonely, trying to find her way, trouble at home, just like the spinster librarian.* "Will you let me check out that book?"

The librarian said, "I'm sorry, Annabeth, but I can't do that. Perhaps if you come back tomorrow, we can talk about this project of yours."

Again a sea change in the girl. She became furtive. "Maybe," she said.

She brushed by the librarian, mounting her backpack as she skipped down the metal circular stairway to the first floor. She was out the front door of the building before Kathy Marks could react.

Absently, the librarian lay *Occult History of Orangefield* in the retrieval cart; Marjorie could put it away tomorrow along with the books she'd neglected.

She was dismounting the spiral staircase, lost in thought, when another series of loud rappings came against the front window.

She froze and stared in that direction.

To the side of one cutout pumpkin, Annabeth Turner's face was pressed against the glass, with the strangest look of triumph and fright. She waved at the librarian and then pulled away from the glass into the night.

The librarian heard a single bark of laughter.

It wasn't until the next day that her assistant Marjorie discovered that three other restricted books, all on the occult, were missing from the LOCAL HISTORY section.

Chapter 2

You've done very well, Wizard.

She wanted to shout, "Thank you!"

Two blocks from the library, on an empty side street, she suddenly became short of breath. A whirling screen of dizzy images replaced her vision as she stopped dead in the street, putting her hands down to the sidewalk to steady herself, trying to calmly regain the flow of air into her lungs.

Faces, twirling pictures in orange and black, pumpkins, always pumpkins, sheeted ghosts like the white sheet she wore when she was little, a bag in her hand, two poke-holes in the eyes, the faces of mother and dead father, his face as white as the sheet, a swirl of candy corn, orange-and-white, a black cat filling her vision with a hiss, red tongue, white teeth and whiskers, green wild eyes and then gone, the steady of the sidewalk suddenly under her hands and her wheezing, throat constricting —

Asthma attack —

She tried to even her breath but it was too late. Knowing from experience not to move, she relaxed and raised one hand from the sidewalk while resting on the other hand and her knees. Slowly she reached around into her pack for the inhaler.

There was no air —

Now panic began to set in. She curled down onto the sidewalk, still rummaging in the bag and then suddenly ripping it off her shoulders, pushing it away from her arms and clawing in the front pocket —

The inhaler wasn't there!

And then suddenly it was — her fingers closing around it and yanking it to her mouth, she was on her back now, staring at streetlights and night sky, the sharp corner of an empty house, and with both hands she pushed the instrument into her mouth, began to breathe in slowly...

Breath came.

Still slowly, she pulled air in, pushing it out in little gasps and then in larger gulps, as the attack subsided.

She waited for him to talk to her, but there was nothing in her head.

She stared at a scattering of stars between the corner of the house and a streetlight, a tall tree limb shorn of most leaves.

As if in answer, an oak leaf pirouetted down into view, landed next to her face.

She wanted to laugh.

And then cry.

"I've done well, haven't I?" she said into the night. "I've done well as Wizard?"

There was no answer.

The house was dark, but that was no surprise.

Annabeth pushed her key into the front door, opened it with a creak. The porch light overhead was off, had been since the bulb had burnt out a month ago. It had gone unreplaced. Just to make sure, she checked the switch on the inside wall — it was off, as she had expected, and when she jiggled it on nothing happened. There was another switch next to the outside light and she flipped it up, which turned on a single lamp on the far side of the living room.

The room was a mess, as always — magazines, newspapers scattered, unpacked boxes, a nest of cat hair on one sidechair where their feline slept, furniture, mantle, a few knick-knacks all undusted. The rug was stained, soiled, hadn't been vacuumed in weeks. Under the single lamp was an ashtray full of cigarette butts, a near-empty tumbler with clear liquid nesting in the bottom, a single ice cube almost extinct.

This is what you get when you have nothing.

With no expectations, Annabeth walked past the stairway, back to the kitchen, which was in similar disarray — stacked dishes, a vague ammonia smell battling the odor of soured milk, a broken dish on the sideboard kept from tumbling into the sink by a half-eaten sandwich perched on the sink's edge, a full garbage can blocking the door to the backyard. The overhead florescent light, a round, naked white curl whose ornamental glass cover had long disappeared, flickered fitfully and never quite blossomed on.

The short hallway behind the kitchen was lined with dust bunnies, two unmatching shoes side by side in the center, incongruous.

Loud snoring came from the bedroom at the end of the hall, the door of which was ajar. As she stopped Annabeth sensed movement, saw Ludwig, their cat, staring out at her balefully from the end of the rumpled bed.

Her mother made an interrupted snorting sound, turned away toward the wall.

Annabeth retreated to the stairway and climbed up to the other bedroom, her own. Within there was another world. The walls were freshly painted, the floors dusted, the throw-rug bright with its original colors. The desk beneath the single window was tidy, one side stacked with schoolbooks, the other, in front of the cane-backed chair, fronted with a clean blotter and a neat row of pens and pencils. The bed was crisply made, covered with a quilt showing a shower of yellow stars and moons against a deep blue background. Over the bed was a single poster, framed, not thumb-tacked, of a white observatory dome, its slit open, revealing the huge telescope within pointed at the night sky. It had been a time-motion shot, the shutter kept open for hours while the stars revolved in the sky, and they formed streaked halos around the dome.

Annabeth's own telescope, a sleek white tube four inches in diameter and nearly three feet long, mounted on a sturdy wooden tripod, stood vigil beside the bed.

Behind it, against the wall, was a bookcase crammed with astronomy books and fantasy novels, as well as a copy of Peter Kerlan's *Sam Hain and the Halloween that Almost Wasn't*.

Annabeth put her backpack on the bed, opened it, and drew out the three stolen library books from inside it. She put them on the blotter on her desk, face down. She leaner over them to look out the window.

Above the huge oak tree in the backyard there was a scattering of stars, but clouds were already moving up from the western horizon into the chill night, and there was a waxing moon still high enough to wash out whatever would be visible.

She could just make out the Great Square of the constellation Pegasus, and, next to it, the constellation Andromeda, which, along its split lines, contained the only galaxy outside the Milky Way visible to the naked eye. She could just make out its faint oval blush. In her telescope, it was a magnificent oval cloud possessing billions of stars far beyond our own galactic neighborhood.

It was said that our own galaxy would someday crash into it.

That, she had decided before coming to Orangefield, was where her dead father's soul was.

Her father's soul, along with all the others, was in the Andromeda Galaxy, which would one day crash into our own galaxy, and bring all the dead back.

That had been her belief.

Now she no longer believed it — but she believed other things instead.

Things that might actually be true.

She turned from the window and looked down at the stack of stolen library books on her blotter.

She turned back to the window and located the Andromeda galaxy again.

"I promise," she said, to the Andromeda galaxy, to her father, to the other billions of souls in that hazy oval of false heaven, "that I'll find you. I promise."

She pulled the shade down over the window, sat down at the desk, and turned over the first book: *Halloween in Orangefield*.

On the front cover had been stamped the word: RESTRICTED.

She opened it; the binding didn't crack, the way an unused book's would; this opening was smooth, the latest of many.

Good, Wizard. Good, the returning voice in her head spoke.

"Everything was fine before he died. You promised—"

And I'll keep my promise, Wizard, if you do what I say.

She smiled to herself and turned the page.

Chapter 3

Perhaps it was the wind that first brought him to the town of Orangefield, a wind that made leaf tornados, dervishing colors from denuded trees. Or perhaps it was the chill in the air, the first cold tendrils of coming winter that were Autumn. Or perhaps it was the children bedecked in Autumn — or the windows with cutouts, or the pumpkins, wet and cold sweet inside, orange, firm and smiling on the outside. Or the season, or the fact that the town had briefly been called Pumpkinfield.

Or perhaps it was because he needed somewhere to serve his Master.

Or maybe it was the evening.

His evening.

Many ways to skin a cat.

Yes, the other voice answered. Indeed. But I am becoming tired of your failed efforts.

This Halloween will be different. I feel the power within me for this. This time I will succeed.

And then? the other voice asked.

And then everything. And I will give it over to you, Dark One.

Do you really think you can do it directly? Without passing through that...other place?

I feel powerful. As powerful as ever.

You've said this before.

This time I have three sure ones to help me. And...

And?

I have what you might call...insurance.

But if, like the last time, one of them fails—

It will succeed.

We shall see.

I am only your servant.

True words. A servant without a choice. I will watch your progress with interest, Samhain.

The voice laughed, a mirthless sound as cold and dead as space.

Or should I call you Sam?

Chapter 4

As far as the eye could see.

The Pumpkin Tender woke up, and was nearly blinded by Autumn colors. There was wetness on his clothes and face, and he shivered as he sat up. The ground had been hard the night before, under the sickle moon, but overnight it had softened beneath him with dew. He had been foolish not to use the Army blanket, one of his only possessions, along with his felt hat and leather boots and his rabbit's foot.

As if to answer his own fear, he reached into his pocket and felt the soft length of the good luck charm. He immediately calmed, enough to rub his eyes and really wake up.

The sun was resting on the Eastern oaks, which meant it was 7:00 A.M. or so. The sky was Autumn blue and cloudless — later the sun would climb and warm the dew back into the air, and it would probably be in the 60s by the afternoon.

He wondered if this would be the day.

He wouldn't have long to find out.

He had chosen to sleep in a low hollow, one of the shallow valleys just outside the town limits, and that had been a foolish thing. He had done many foolish things lately, which vaguely bothered him. Some of the memories crowded into his head, and he pushed them out, physically driving them back with his hands, making agitated sounds with his mouth.

He closed his eyes and the memories were gone.

Frankenstein, the kids in Orangefield called him, because he was big and wore shabby clothes and had rough hands and could no longer talk.

Not since—

Again he became agitated, and looked to the sun for help. It was above the trees now, free of them, climbing. In another hour or two it would show him what he lived to see.

The only thing he lived for.

That and the other thing...

The worst memory of all came into his head and now he cried out, making the same sounds Frankenstein made in that movie he saw before the Army. He could speak, then, and walk without a bad hitch in his right leg. Sometimes he almost had clear memories of the way he had been before the Army, when he drove a '64 Mustang convertible which he'd restored himself, and smoked cigarettes and drank beer and was on the bowling team at Ace's and there was the girl Peggy...

His loud sounds turned to mewling and he sat down facing the sun. He found his Army blanket at his feet and pulled it up around him.

He had been another man before the Army. The training he remembered, Fort Bragg, shipping out, Somalia, but all of it was speeded up like a fast-motion film with a cartoon *whirring* sound which got higher and higher pitched until it stopped dead on the moment his foot was resting on the anti-personnel mine and froze there, his eyes looking down and his brain screaming *What the hell?* even as his weight lifted off the mine and it went off, and his leg, his thigh, his hip was blown to bits.

He knew that wasn't quite right, that there was more, but he couldn't quite remember...

He had a feeling if he did it would make things even worse.

Felt like someone tearing the meat off my bones was the last rational thought he had before a piece of his own ankle bone ripped into his mouth and then up through his palate, severing his tongue on the way, stopping in his brain.

"Kid made his own bullet," one of the field doctors said later, laughing in that sardonic, funeral parlor way MASH doctors had, and even now part of him wanted to laugh the same way when he remembered that.

Then he came home and after a while was *Frankenstein*.

No more Peggy, no siree, not with three-quarters of a brain and no tongue and a hitch in his walk bigger than Festis on TV...

He watched the sun climb ever higher — he'd know when it was time — but already he felt it warming the wet off him, inside his blanket.

No more Aaron Peters, he'd had a tongue and a good leg and a girlfriend and a car and liked to read history books. A pretty good pitching arm, too, and not a bad quarterback for a lefty.

He became, instead, Frankenstein.

And the Pumpkin Tender.

Peggy married a guy named Turk, who laid a hand on her now and then, he heard someone say. The same someone said it was a shame, that Aaron would have made a wonderful husband.

Maybe it was his mother who said that, he wasn't sure...

No more bowling, his kid brother took the Mustang and wrapped it around a pole six months later, walking away from the wreck but in a way The Pumpkin Tender was glad the car was gone. One thing less to think about when he looked at it, memories firing off like pistons in his broken head.

He knew they were uncomfortable when he was home so he'd started staying away as much as he could, and that took care of their guilt at least in the summer and fall when old Joshua Froelich hired him to weed and tend his pumpkin patch.

"Better'n a dog," Froelich had said, since Aaron tended Froelich's land like a hawk on legs, killing anything — weed, insect, or animal — that went after the pumpkins. Soon word about this wonder had spread, and The Pumpkin Tender found himself taking care of most of the pumpkins in Orangefield. In the winter he stayed mostly at home, making them all nervous and irritable, becoming Frankenstein, but in the spring, after the last snow, he began to wander the still-fallow fields which surrounded the town like a wreath, pulling up rocks which had been forced up through the frozen ground, cleaning out dead vines and late weeds he had missed the previous Autumn, making his fields ready for planting. By the time planting came in summer he lived in the fields, tending each shoot like a baby and nurturing each budded fruit as if it was the only one in the world. The pumpkins he tended were the best grown, the cleanest, the fattest, brightest-colored, longest-lasting-after-picking, finest in all of the Northeast. Froelich, and the other growers, had customers drive two hundred miles just to buy one of those pumpkins.

The Pumpkin Tender had become indispensable.

And, perhaps, today would be the one day in the year he would be truly happy.

He thought it might be. The way the sun was rising, the cleanness of the atmosphere, the warm/cold snap in the air, gave him hope. It would have to be today, because he felt rain behind this weather, which meant that if tomorrow was the day he would lose it.

He stood up.

No, today was the day. He was sure.

He left the Army blanket in a heap and began the long, limping trek to the High Spot. He didn't think about this. Like an animal drawn to a spawning ground, he took step after step toward his goal.

His leg began to ache after a half hour, but he ignored it. He passed Froelich's farm-stand, passing behind the building so he wouldn't have to interact with the old man — but Froelich was in the back, unloading potato sacks from the back of his pickup truck.

"This the day, Aaron?" the old man said, stopping his work. He was overweight and already perspiring.

Aaron nodded curtly and limped on.

There was an understanding tone in Froelich's voice. "Maybe I'll join you up there later, after you've been alone with it awhile."

The Pumpkin Tender made a sound in the back of his throat, and kept walking. Froelich had never joined him, and was just being polite.

The sun was higher now, and the sky was a achingly clear blue. The chill had dissipated. It would be even warmer than he thought — maybe up into the low 70s.

He brought his felt hat off his head with his left hand, mopped his sweaty face with it and pushed it back onto his head.

The ground was now steadily ascending.

Already if he turned around he would be above the valleys which surrounded Orangefield. Beyond those valleys were either softly rolling hills or a few higher spots, only one of which could be considered a mountain. It wasn't tall enough to be named, but was high enough to afford a view of the entire area.

Halfway up the mountain, and by his reading of the sun just before noon, he stopped. His leg from the hip to his rebuilt ankle was on fire. He sat down in a hollow under a tree; the spot was filled with red and gold leaves and he was able to nest down into it and stretch his leg out.

He was thirsty and hungry, and had neither food or water. There was a stream a little way on but he had been warned not to drink from it — the one time he had done so his stomach had been turned inside-out for three days.

The red and gold leaves reminded him of fire, as if his leg was burning in them.

Abruptly the leaves began to remind him of flames, of burning up his leg and the ripping sound of his own flesh being torn away, and he reached down and brushed all the leaves away from his legs.

He was facing away from the sun.

His leg began to feel better, a lessening of the fire, and he lay back and became comfortable in the warmth and the lessening of pain.

He closed his eyes, and soon fell asleep.

He dreamed, and for once the dream was almost a pleasant one to begin with, blue and white and he was in the clouds, flying above a flaming earth, none of the heat reaching him, it was cool and he was comfortable and floated with no effort or fear.

And then the world below him went suddenly dark and the fires went away without leaving smoke, and the clouds were gone and the sky around him became darker and darker, and he was surrounded by black and cold and was falling, trying to scream and nothing came out—

He awoke with a start, and called out from his ruined mouth. For a moment he was disoriented. He heard a crackling sound, and felt leaves behind his head, and saw his legs in the cleared-out spot.

He became very agitated — the light around him was deeper than it should be.

Alarmed, he stood up, feeling a fresh hot bolt of pain through his leg. He ignored it. He hobbled out of the hollow spot, onto the path again, and faced the sun.

It was past its height, and moving down in its arc toward the west in the late of day. And, in the west, clouds were already forming on the line of the horizon, rising like yeast to meet the approaching sun.

He had slept for hours.

He wanted to cry. He had missed the height of the sun.

Steeling himself, he turned to the upward path and limped onto it.

Perhaps it was not too late.

His leg quickly became a pure hot pain with each step. He gritted his teeth and ignored it. After a while he heard an anguished sound which fell into step with him — he realized the cries were his own loud grunts at the pace he'd set.

But he could now see the summit above him, growing closer with each burning step.

He came around a curve in the path, circum-venting a stand of already denuded trees, and saw the flat top of the mountain a matter of twenty yards ahead.

His leg folded under him, and he fell.

A sound like a strangled cry came from his mouth. His leg felt as if it had been dipped into acid.

He tried to get up, but fell back again.

The sun was descending toward the west, darkening with late autumn day — soon it would be twilight.

He tried again to rise, and failed.

He began to sob.

Suddenly there were hands beneath his armpits, pulling him up.

"Can't have you missin' your favorite day of the year, can we, Aaron?"

He was on his feet, and supported. He turned to see old Froelich's face next to his own.

The old man looked suddenly embarrassed at the intimacy, and turned away. But his grip on Aaron was like iron. "Don't worry 'bout it, son. Just thought you were in an extra bit of difficulty with the leg this year, when you went by the stand. Thought it was time I see this sight myself, anyways. So I took the truck up as far as I could, walked the rest. Thought you'd be up and gone by now. And if you weren't..." He shrugged, looked Aaron in the face again.

"Let's have us a look, shall we?" Froelich said.

With the old man's help, the Pumpkin Tender suddenly found himself on the top of the mountain, looking down at the valleys which surrounded Orangefield — the scores of pumpkin fields and patches which merged into an orange circle, a ring of fire, the sight of thousands of unpicked pumpkins in the late sun. It was even more magnificent than it would have been at noon — the deep tone of setting Sol making the fields seem to be lit from within.

"Well I'll be damned, I will," old Froelich said in amazement. "I had no idea it would be this beautiful, Aaron. And it's all your doing, boy. All those clean, beautiful pumpkins...." He laughed. "Hell, we could sell tickets to this, it's so beautiful."

There were tears in the Pumpkin Tender's eyes. His mouth opened and a little gasping sound came out.

"That's all right, son," Froelich said, tightening his grip under Aaron's arms. "You just stand there and enjoy it. Hell, it's gonna rain tomorrow, and then the picking will start. This'll all be gone for another year."

The sun sank into imperceptible twilight, and the ring of fire's glow faded, like cooling embers.

"I'll be damned," the old farmer repeated, his voice fading like the light.

They stood together silently for a moment; the sun dropped into the clouded horizon, and the glow disappeared, dying light.

"Come on, son," Froelich said, trying to urge the Pumpkin Tender to turn away. "Time we went back down. The truck's just a little ways down the path."

Aaron wouldn't move. There were tears on his face, and his weight caused the old man to let go of his grip and gently lower him to the ground.

"Gonna stay up here tonight, Aaron?" Froelich asked. He knew from experience not to try to fight the Pumpkin Tender's impulses. "All right, then. Just in case, I went and got your spare Army blanket from the spot in the shed where you keep your stuff. It's in the truck, let me get it."

The old man wandered off down the path, returned a few minutes later.

Aaron, on the ground, his legs folded awkwardly, felt the blanket go around his shoulders.

"You take care up here, boy. Try to rest that leg of yours."

Aaron heard the old man's steps retreat, heard the rumbling roar of the truck's engine a few moments later — the protesting grind of changed gears, the crunch of tires turning. Headlights stabbed through the growing dark above his head, arced away. In a moment he heard the truck change gears again, the fading sound of its engine as it made its rumbling way down the mountain.

He was alone with the coming night. Already the line of clouds in the west had eaten the sun, were climbing up the sky, eating away early stars.

The ring of fire around Orangefield, which now blinked on its own electric lights against the night, was gone.

Tears continued to dry on the Pumpkin Tender's face.

His hands beneath the blanket gripped and ungripped.

Inside his head the voice, the same voice which had been talking to him since Froelich had lifted him up, had continued to talk to him insistently, soothingly, with command, as he had tried to enjoy the ring of fire of his own making, still talked to him. It was the clearest thing he had heard since Somalia, and he knew if it kept up he would listen to it—

Remember me? it said.

Chapter 5

Lists.

While he buried the headless animal, Jordie thought about all the lists he kept. There was the comic book list — his favorites, beginning with *The Fantastic Four* and ending, at the very bottom, with *Batman*. There was a lot in between but *Batman* was the only D.C. title in the bunch, and just barely. He had liked the movies more than the books, but there was something about the character that he just couldn't dismiss. Maybe it was the fact that Batman was just a man with a neat suit. No super powers, no glowing rocks, no fast-motion — just a man with a mission.

Man with a mission.

Jordie kept lots of other lists: lists of what to get at the store, of what parts he needed to order for his turntables — needles, especially, he needed new needles for his cartridges, his vinyl was starting to sound a bit distorted — a list of what needed to be done around the house. That was the one he hated the most — but one, now that he thought about it, that he didn't have to bother with anymore. Mom and Aunt Binny had worked long and hard on that one — but, well, he just wouldn't bother with it anymore.

The animal's torso was covered with dirt; he wondered idly if he'd dug deep enough but decided that, hell, that sounded too much like a chore so what he'd done was good enough.

"You don't work, you don't go to school, you don't do anything around the house—" his mother was fond of saying.

"Look, Ma, I'm doin' a chore!" he answered, giggling.

Man, it was cold. He looked down at himself and saw that he was naked, smeared with blood. The sun had gone down. It had still been up when he started digging, but now it was dark and getting chilly. He stood up, dropped the shovel and dusted his hands, turning toward the house.

Lists.

There was something else he was supposed to do.

He looked down on the ground, looking for the list, but couldn't locate it.

He shrugged, walked into the house, turning lights on as he went. He had a joint somewhere,

where was it? He couldn't remember. He vaguely remembered smoking three or four in the morning, afternoon. And there had been a pint of Scotch in there somewhere, or had it been a fifth...

The house was a mess, kitchen chairs turned over, table on its side, blood smears on the white floors, walls, refrigerator, everywhere. The head of a cat stared at him from the kitchen counter, next to the toaster oven. Another, larger head was next to it. A second animal, what looked like a mouse but was actually a squirrel, lay eviscerated on the toaster oven's open door.

He laughed at the mouse/cat thing.

The rest of the house, living and dining room, was a mess, too — some broken furniture, the couch with a burn mark in the center cushion, a scatter of feathers in the fireplace —

The bathroom, at least, was clean.

He took a slow shower, letting warm and then hot water sluice over him, scrubbing himself with Ivory soap. He still couldn't remember what the other list had said. He knew he should, but his head was just too cloudy —

He let hot, steamy water run into his face, onto his shaggy head of hair.

Got to remember, got to —

It almost came to him, then danced off into the back of his mind again. Finally he shut off the water with an angry, squeaky turn of the handle, got out of the shower and stood before the mirror.

Lettered on the steamed surface in a bold hand was: IN YOUR ROOM.

"Yeah?" he said, out loud.

Then, in his head, the voice fighting through all the static: *Go to your room, Jodie.*

He shrugged. "Whatever."

Not bothering to towel himself off, he padded out of the bathroom, pushing aside a broken end table that had somehow found its way in front of his bedroom, and opened the door.

The usual mess inside, nothing more: unmade bed, vinyl records scattered on the floor, a pair of Timberlake boots in front of the open, cluttered closet, his turntables neat and clean on their industrial-sized folding table flanking stacked amp and mixer, huge JBL dj speakers to either side on the carpeted floor.

He switched the rig on — forgetting about the voice, the list.

The amp hummed into life, and he opened the turn covers; one already had an lp on it, gangster rap, and he slapped an r&b record pulled at random from the nearest sleeve onto the other.

He let the rap record dash into its angry opening, then abruptly switched over with the mixer to the mild rhythm and blues record. Snorting satisfaction, he kept it there, a soft crooning voice flowing from the excellent speakers.

"Awwright!"

Find the list, Jordie.

"Right. Sure."

And there it was, right in front of him, on top of the amp, taped down and neat as can be. Next to it was another piece of paper which looked older, folded over and taped closed.

At the bottom of the list was: *Mom*, followed by *Aunt Binny*, then a list of large animals ascending to *Cat* and *Squirrel* at the top.

So that had been what he was burying — the cat's body.

Rusty, his name was.

Had been.

You didn't listen to me, Jordie.

Jordie shrugged, hardly listening; he was mouthing the words of the R&B song.

You didn't follow my directions.

The needle abruptly scratched all the way across the surface of the vinyl, then lifted by itself and was set firmly in its cradle.

Jordie watched this in horror, complained, "Hey! Those things cost money!"

The amp switched itself off.

Listen to me, Jordie.

"Bullshi—"

The electrical cord from the amp pulled itself from the back of the machine, frayed into two separate wires, touched Jordie's still dripping leg.

A shock went through him, up his body into his neck.

He found himself on the floor, trembling, a red raw welt on his leg where the wires had touched.

Listen.

"Yeah. Okay." His voice was weak, suddenly frightened.

Get dressed.

"Sure. Whatever you say."

Yes, Jordie, whatever I say. From now on.

He dressed quickly, jeans, shirt, Timberlakes.

Take the list. Go into the living room.

Head clear now, hands still trembling, Jordie reached for the taped, closed list on the amp.

Not that one. The first one.

"Sure." Jodie took the original list.

Now go into the living room and clean up.

"Right." He stumbled out of his bedroom, down the hall and into the living room.

His mother's headless body was in front of the couch, his Aunt Binny's body sprawled in a wing chair facing the fireplace.

You were supposed to start at the top of the list, Jordie. Not the bottom.

"Huh?"

And I told you to spread it out over the next few days, ease into it slowly.

"Really?"

I didn't expect you to be so... eager — and so fast.

52

Jordie shrugged idly. "Whatever."

That's not good enough. I'm going to give you a second chance, but I want you to do everything I say. Do you agree?

Jordie heard the sound of something sliding up the hallway, looked to see the electrical cord, two bare wires poised like a coiled python in the opening to the living room. The other end of the cord slid into view like a snake and plugged itself with a *snick* into a wall outlet just inside the room.

"Gottcha. Whatever you say."

Go back into your bedroom and look at the second list taped to your amp.

"Sure. Right away."

Jordie moved out of the room, giving the electrical cord a wide berth — its bare-wired ends, like slitted copper eyes hanging in the air, followed his movements.

He stumbled backwards into his room, went to the amp and pulled off the second list.

Open it up.

"No problem."

The electrical cord had followed him, was in the doorway, watching.

He opened the piece of paper, stared at it. It had been folded many times, was creased through some of the writing, which had faded it. Its edges were frayed. It was in a different hand than the other list, which, now that he concentrated on it, he remembered writing himself.

Read it, Jordie. Out loud.

This one was in his mother's hand. He remembered that now, the careful penmanship, she had written this note for him a long time ago.

Read it now, Jordie. The voice was impatient.

"Remember to take your meds, Jordie," he read. "Remember the doses." Then there was a list underneath, various doses each of various pills, names like *Clozaril, Zoloft, Lithium, Zyprexa*, as well as the times he needed to take them:

The note was signed, "Love, Mom."

I want you to begin to take your meds again, Jordie. Only in slightly different doses.

"But you told me to stop—"

Yes. And now I want you to start again, in the doses I tell you to take. They'll make you...receptive and happy. And now I want you to clean up. I want you to clean up so no one will know.

"Sure thing."

I'll tell you how to take your meds from now on.

He held up the note in his hand. "But...but my Mom—"

Just listen to me from now on. You don't need that list anymore. Get rid of it. From now on I'll make lists for you.

Jordie stared at the note in his hand for a moment — *Love, Mom* — and then crumpled it up and let it drop to the floor.

Very good, Jordie.

Jordie saw with relief that the electrical cord had dropped to the hallway floor and lay curled and dead.

When you're finished cleaning up, the voice said, *I want you to sleep. Then I'll have a new list for you. Tomorrow, you can decorate the house for Halloween.*

Chapter 6

On page 21 of the second of the three books she had stolen from the Orangefield Library, *A Short History of Halloween*, Annabeth Turner found what she was looking for:

Samhain, the Celtic Lord of Death — whose celebration day was also known as Samhain — had the power to return the souls of the dead to their earthly homes for one evening — the evening which eventually became known in the Christian era as All Hallows Eve.

So that's who he was: *Call me Sam*.

She looked up from the book out through the window over her desk but there was no answer.

She turned back to the book.

She knew she had only tonight to learn whatever she could from the three books. *Halloween in Orangefield* had proved useless: the usual local historian twaddle, written to titillate visitors and tourists without telling them anything of historical import. It was little more than a children's book, and she wondered why it had been in the restricted area at all.

A Short History of Halloween must have been placed in the Local History section by mistake, but had proved at least of some use — but besides its discussion of the Celts, and their Lord of Death, it had quickly veered away into modern practices.

She put it aside, and opened the third book.

The spine cracked with disuse — she wondered if she was the first to ever open the book and saw by the librarian's card in the front that it had never been taken out.

Occult Practises in Orangefield and Chicawa County, New York, 1668-1940.

She looked at the copyright page, and saw that it had only recently been published, and that a second volume, covering 1941 to the present, was promised by the publisher, who was also the author: T. R. Reynolds.

She turned to the first page of text.

Immediately she was disappointed — it was illustrated with a picture of the Salem witch trials, a solemn woodcut of three witches being burned at the stake. Annabeth was a good, fast reader, and skimmed through the accompanying description of the Salem hysteria; her eyes stopped when she reached the following:

It isn't generally recognized that a similar episode of hysteria occurred in Orangefield, New York, the previous spring, predating the Salem madness by almost a year. What makes the Orangefield episode doubly interesting — and makes it doubly curious that it has for so long been ignored — is that a total of fourteen women and three men were condemned as agents of the devil, and that ten of them in all — eight of the women and two men — were executed either by hanging or stoning. Perhaps because none were burned at the stake this episode has been generally forgotten, both in local lore and in the larger picture of witch hysteria which gripped the eastern colonies during that short, strange period.

Annabeth skimmed ahead, flying past numerous supposed "possessions" and, during the Civil War, a mass disappearance of local men which the author tried to relate to an earlier Virginia episode but which turned out to be a mass avoidance of Union Army conscription.

The rest of the book, as she moved through it quickly, looked to be composed of similar stories, many of which were backed up by nothing but hearsay and gossip.

She was about to give up on the book when she moved to the last chapter: THE PUMPKINFIELD ERA AND THE BEGINNING OF 'SAMHAIN SIGHTINGS.'

The chapter was fronted by a black and white photograph of a field of pumpkins, row after row nearly to the horizon, with a caption that read: *First pumpkin farm in 'Pumpkinfield,' 1940.*

Once again she skimmed, learning that, during the early part of the Great Depression, the name of the town, as a publicity gimmick, had been briefly changed to Pumpkinfield. When the name change produced little increase in tourist traffic, it was changed back to Orangefield. By this time word had spread about the size and quality of the local pumpkins, and this, more than any gimmick, is what finally made the town prosperous.

But by 1940, after the town had regained its original name, a curious phenomenon had begun: sightings, around Halloween, of a dark, cloaked figure appearing in pumpkin fields, usually at night, which the locals dubbed 'Samhain Sightings.' There didn't seem to be any specific origin for the sightings, and the author had, by his own admission, been unable to discover why the name Samhain had become attached to the mysterious figure.

There followed the same short description of the Celtic Death Lord, the pagan rituals which had attended him on All Hallows Eve, which *A Short History of Halloween* had provided.

But then there was this:

In October of 1941, just before the onset of World War II, there occurred in Orangefield an unprecedented rash of sightings of what the locals now referred to as 'Sam.' Up until that point the name had been used with an almost cheerful irreverence (see notes, pp. 124-126, interviews with Mattie Michaels, etc.) which mirrored that of the residents of Loch Ness, in Scotland, who affectionately call their lake creature Nessie. But after the incidents of 1941 things changed, and to this day the name Samhain is rarely spoken of lightly in Orangefield, even in jest. It is rare to hear the phenomenon referred to as Sam any more. Indeed, during the writing of the present volume, the author became aware of the mysterious death of the children's horror author Peter Kerlan, an Orangefield resident who, just before his demise (the mystery of which will be covered in a later volume of this history) revived the name 'Sam' for a series of children's books on Samhain, only one of which was written. It is not known if Kerlan was even aware of Sam's earlier incarnation at the time of his death.

Annabeth glanced at her own copy of *Sam Hain and the Halloween that Almost Wasn't* in her bookcase, before turning back to T.R. Reynolds's history.

There followed a few descriptions of early Sam sightings, usually of a tall, darkly cloaked, unspeaking figure which appeared in the middle of a pumpkin patch on moonlit nights; the sightings became more numerous as Halloween approached, and continued even after a prankster from a nearby town was caught 'impersonating' Samhain.

Even this, Reynolds admits, might have ended the matter if two grizzly murders hadn't occurred on Halloween of that year; the bodies, of a teenaged girl and boy, had been found hacked to pieces in a pumpkin patch. There were unidentified shoe prints near the bodies, and the murders were never solved.

After that, the name Sam, or Samhain, was rarely spoken of at all in Orangefield. The murders, allied to other strange occurrences that fall and Winter, which was a harsh one, conspired to turn Sam from a local legend into something taboo. There were economic as well as cultural reasons for this, no doubt — if people were scared of a black-cloaked murderer, they wouldn't come to Orangefield for the pumpkins or the foliage, and they wouldn't spend their money there. That, and the fact that Pearl Harbor was bombed five weeks after Halloween and the murders, which turned local interests to more solid and national pursuits. Indeed by the end of the war, the 'Sam' phenomenon had all but been forgotten, and there were no more sightings until 1951, a period which will be discussed in the second volume of this history, which will also cover the bizarre occurances surrounding Orangefield's annual Pumpkin

Days Festival, held every year during the week leading up to Halloween, and which was initiated in 1952.

The book abruptly ended at that point, leaving Annabeth both satisfied and frustrated. She wanted to know more — wanted to know *all* of it. She searched in vain for some indication of when the second volume would be published, but found nothing — there wasn't even a picture of the author on the back cover.

She turned to the copyright page again, noting the publisher's address: Reynolds Publishing, 1420 Acre Street, Orangefield. She wrote it down.

Sleep tugged at her, and she readied for bed and slipped under the covers. The room was cold, and she pulled the star-covered quilt up to her chin. Tomorrow she would return the three books to the library when Ms. Marks, the librarian, wasn't there. She'd learned everything she could from the library, anyway.

You're doing well, Wizard.

The voice was in her head, just as it had been at the library this afternoon. There was almost laughter in it.

"Sam? Is that you?" she whispered.

Perhaps. We'll meet when the time is right. Be patient.

"But I want to know everything! I want—"

We all want things. There are things you will do for me. Then you will get what you want, as I promised.

In the dark, she felt the most insubstantial caress of fingers across her face. She reached out but there was nothing there, the merest hint of smoke. The fingers touched her own, grasping them for a fraction of a second before the smoke melted away.

The faintest of kisses brushed her lips — she smelled nutmeg and allspice, a hint of cloves. There was almost a face, white and wide, shimmering, deep sockets with no eyes, a mouth opened in an oval grin which puffed apart into mist.

Soon, Wizard...

"You promised—"

There were tears on her face, sobs threatening to well up within her.

I know what I promised, the voice said. *Go to sleep.*

"I want to know where he is..."

She closed her eyes and slept a dreamless sleep.

PART TWO
Pumpkin Days

Chapter 7

Pumpkins.

Everywhere pumpkins.

Orangefield became an orange town.

If you had watched from the sky, you would have seen a remarkable thing. On October 1st, Orangefield was surrounded by a glorious ring of orange, a corona of pumpkin patches and cultivated fields, fruit so clean and bright they seemed to glow. And then on October 2nd the ring began to contract, the farthest layers melting inward toward the town itself. The farthest fields were picked first, fat pumpkins suddenly appearing on farm stand shelves and PICK YOUR OWN PUMPKIN signs springing up like toadstools on roadsides. And the ring continued to contract. By the second week in October it was half as thick as it had been, and now orange began to fill the town of Orangefield.

By October 14th the ring was all but gone, a few spots of orange, a rotted or trampled pumpkin here and there, a few that grew too small to pick, or too large and oddly shaped to sell. The farm stands were bursting with fruit now, the roadside stands top-heavy with pumpkins — glorious round fat fruit that *smelled* orange.

And Orangefield was filled with pumpkins.

Pumpkins everywhere.

By the morning of the 15th, the beginning of Pumpkin Days, Orangefield from the air was as orange as its corona of pumpkin fields had been. There was orange everywhere. Every house had a porchful of pumpkins — on some houses, the foundations all the way around the house were lined with orange fruit. Every mailbox had a pumpkin guarding its post; backyards and front were guarded by scarecrows with pumpkin heads. Every front window was filled with pumpkin cutouts; each door bore another, larger cardboard pumpkin face.

In Rainer Park, in the middle of town, the viewing stand was draped in orange bunting. The pumpkin floats would parade by here and, behind the grandstand were the tables lined with hundreds of the best pumpkins for the carving competition. The telephone poles were topped with plastic pumpkins; City Hall sported its orange and white banner proclaiming *WELCOME   PUMPKIN   DAYS FESTIVAL!* And under it: the mayor's name in as bold letters as he dared display. He would ride the first float and open the ceremonies himself.

And more pumpkins.

And more.

An orange stripe down Main Street, in washable paint. And Orange Men, the gaggle of college students who spray-painted themselves orange each year; one, after too much beer, inevitably used real paint. And orange costumes — the best imitation of a pumpkin, various grades. The school projects displayed at the circumference of the park: the science of pumpkin growing, things made with pumpkins (a pair of shoes!), hundreds of uses for pumpkins.

Then the baked goods and recipe displays — pumpkin cake and bread, and pies of course, and cookies and pumpkin ale (the college students, again) and pumpkin milk and pumpkin juice. An entire meal made of pumpkin, from something resembling chicken (strips of rind from near the skin, boiled in chicken stock and then broiled) and something else resembling mashed potatoes, and things that looked like carrots and cucumbers and even peas, with pumpkin tea and pumpkin ice cream for dessert. Pumpkin ravioli, and soup, and sausage. Pumpkin pancakes, waffles. Pumpkin french toast, made with pumpkin bread.

Orange everywhere.

Pumpkins everywhere.

Pumpkin Days, Orangefield in its glory — with attendant tourist dollars.

From the decimated corona, the battlefield after the war, the now fallow fields surrounding Orangefield, the Pumpkin Tender heard the celebrations, muted. He never attended the festival, had never even thought much of it before Somalia. Now, he stayed away as a religion. There were his trampled fields to tend, the forgotten fruit, too small or too large or too strange, which had been left behind.

This was one of his favorite times, after the viewing of the orange corona. He had been in hiding since October 2nd, while the violence had been done, and now he was left alone to fix the damage.

And collect his own special pumpkins.

He didn't mind the strange-shaped fruit, the elongated shapes that resembled huge orange eggplants, the too-thin, the tiny, the massive squat shapes that looked like hassocks. The double-pumpkins, twins growing together. Even triplets, attached at the same stem.

All day he collected them from the various fields, and brought them all to one of Froelich's smaller patches. And always, as the day wore on, the raucous sounds coming from Orangefield and its Pumpkin Days.

By nightfall he had nearly filled the small patch with these freak fruits, and had enough to create a miniature of the fields he had tended for so many months.

In Orangefield, the lights went on, the festival continued: the night parade, the march of the pumpkins, more eating, more judging.

The glow from the town made the Pumpkin Tender's patch glow with an orange warmth. The moon, waxing fat, rose in back of the field, giving a colder light. The Pumpkin Tender sat down in front of his patch, and pulled his Army blanket around him, and rested quietly.

There was a large pumpkin in front of him, which had not been picked but had been growing in this patch; it was deformed into two lobes near the bottom but the upper part was perfect, round and firm with a strong life-giving vine still in the ground. He would keep this one alive until Thanksgiving, at least.

But now, abruptly, there was something wrong with it.

Though it hadn't been picked, somehow it had been carved, and now sported a two-toothed grin, triangle eyes and nose.

A fire, not moonlight, flared up within it, and the smile widened.

"Time for us to talk, Aaron," it said.

Behind it, in the middle of the patch, something dark rose up from the ground — cloaked, tall, with a hidden face.

The Pumpkin Tender looked at the fat, lobed, still-growing pumpkin again — it was back to normal, had no carved face, was smooth and untouched.

Time for us to talk.

This time the voice came from the dark-cloaked figure, which was suddenly closer, standing over him. It smelled cold, like the night, and, faintly, like pumpkin pie spice.

Aaron remembered the voice — it was the *Remember me?* voice.

He remembered other things, which he didn't want to...

You haven't listened to me yet, the voice said, *but now I think you will.*

And the cloak covered him.

And he screamed.

Chapter 8

"Did you notice anything weird at Jordie's house?" Will Coppel asked. He drained the last drops from his fifth beer and crushed the can, dropping it into the pile in the midst of the four boys.

The other three laughed, and Josh Hammer said, "Weird? That dude is *always* weird. Always was."

Will fished behind him into the cooler, felt his hand slip into bone-chilling water as he searched for another beer. His hand hit one, two beers and he snagged the third as it swam by.

"I'm not joking," he said as he popped the tab. "You know how Jordie has to keep all those medications he takes balanced. He's acting like they're all screwed up. And by the way, we're almost out of beer."

A collective groan went up. Behind them, inside the Music Festival tent, a circus-sized temporary structure at one end of Rainer Park, rap music burst into the night again; the break was over, and now it was the turn of the third and fourth of their group to groan again and go back inside and help the DJ.

One of them turned before climbing under the tent flap. "That leaves you two to get more brews," he said.

Josh pushed the cooler into a hidden spot beneath some nearby bushes, and stood up. "Forget driving," he said, "I've had too many."

"Me too," Will replied. "Got your i.d.?"

Josh fished in the front pocket of his pants, produced a card. "Phony as Dolly Parton's tits," he laughed. "I can't believe we're twenty years old and can't buy a beer without lying about it."

"Let's walk to Burrita's," Will replied. He glanced blurrily at his watch. "Ten to eleven. He's open till midnight, right?"

"I don't remember," Josh answered. "Might be eleven tonight."

They set off through the park, in the direction of the main road. The night was still misty with the remnants of the night's fireworks display; there would be another on the last night of Pumpkin Days, next Saturday. In between, there would be nightly music in the tent. Tonight it was rap music's turn;

another night, classical, with the high school band filling in another night and a polka party yet another.

"You ever think about how stupid all this Pumpkin Days crap is?" Josh laughed.

"Bullshit. You've loved it since you were a kid. It's one of the best things about this town."

His friend snorted in agreement.

Will went on, "I wasn't kidding about Jordie being fucked up."

"You think he stopped taking his pills?"

Will didn't laugh. "Maybe," he said, nodding back toward the tent, which was now in the distance behind them. A Puff Daddy song, its lyrics cleaned of numerous obscenities, could barely be heard.

Josh snorted again. They had reached Main Street and waited for traffic to clear in front of them, cars still pulling away from the end of the fireworks display, others trying to park to catch some of the music in the tent. It was a little colder than it had been, and Will suddenly shivered.

"Don't know about his meds," Josh answered, "but he's as big a weedhead as ever. I noticed him pull a pint bottle from his pants during his first set, too."

"That's part of what I'm talking about. When he's on his medication, Jordie's even-tempered. Mild and funny as hell and wouldn't hurt a fly. Remember all that crazy stuff he used to do in grade school, just to make us laugh? And that time he flipped out when we found that puppy that had been hit by a car?"

"He cried like it had been his."

Will's face darkened, and he nodded his head. "And remember that time in seventh grade when he didn't take his pills, just to see what would happen?"

There was an opening in the traffic, and Josh dashed out into the street, Will after him. They reached the other side and began to walk quickly; Will checked his watch — it was within five to eleven.

"You bet your ass I remember," Will said, quickening his pace. "Tore up a classroom and almost killed old Peterson. They were going to throw him out — *shit*."

They had stopped abruptly in front of a convenience store with the name *Burrita's* over it; the lights within were out and the hours posted in the window stated that they closed at 7:00 on Sundays.

"I forgot what day it was," Will said. "We won't find anything open now."

"Just as well," Josh laughed; he had reached into his wallet and found it empty. "And I know you haven't got more than a buck on you," he continued, "you cheap bastard."

"Let's go back."

They reversed their steps, crossing to the other side of Main Street as soon as they could and straddling the park fence till they came to the entrance.

The tent glowed from within, and they could see shadows of the dancers moving in strange shapes across the canvas surface.

"Looks cool," Josh said. He glanced at Will. "So spit it out. I can tell there's still something on your mind."

"It was just too normal in Jordie's house tonight. Everything looked like it had been cleaned, just for us. You know his Mom and his Aunt—"

"She ain't really his Aunt, dude."

"That's just a rumor—"

"Jordie told me himself. It's why his father left. Jordie didn't seem to give a crap, one way or the other—"

"Well, anyway, I don't ever remember the house being all that clean. Tonight it looked like it had been scrubbed. And when I asked him about all the Halloween decorations in the windows, he laughed and said he put them there himself. Can you see Jordie taking the time to do something like that?"

Now Will laughed. "No way. He's a bigger slacker than you or me."

"There was just something weird in that house, is all."

"And why do you care?"

For the first time that evening Will looked at his friend in a completely sober way. "It's just that I think we should be responsible for our friends, is all. If we're not, why bother to have friends?"

Josh studied his face for a moment, then broke out in a grin. "Man, we've got to find you another beer!" he said. "You're *way* too serious!"

At midnight, the last record was played, with one of the local sheriff's deputies politely telling Jordie, with Josh and Will helping him by this time, that it was time to call it a night. The deputy, whose name was Charlie Fredricks, and who wasn't much older than Will, was a good guy and whispered to Will, "Tell your friend Jordie to leave the bottle home next time, or I'll have to bust him. He's been acting weird all night, and, from what I hear, for the last week or so. I've already told him I'm gonna keep an eye on him." He slapped Will lightly on the back and walked away.

The music ended, the crowd left, and they broke down the equipment in short order, pulling out cables, stacking the amp and turntables, slipping the vinyl LPS which littered the table and ground into their paper sleeves, their album covers, and then into the plastic milk crates that held them. Will and Josh carried the heavy speakers out first, hauling them by their handles and handling them into the bed of Josh's truck.

By twelve thirty they were completely packed, and on their way back to Jordie's house.

In the closed cab of the truck they could smell the overpowering sweetness of Jordie's breath.

"Say, Jordie, how much Scotch did you drink?" Josh asked, adding the deputy's warning.

"Fuck 'im," Jordie grinned, pulled an empty pint bottle from the deep leg pocket of his baggy pants, let it fall to the floor. He giggled, pulling another empty pint from the other leg pocket, also empty. He frowned momentarily, then reached into his jacket pocket and produced a third bottle, three-quarters full. He unscrewed the top and took a pull.

"Jesus, you're gonna kill yourself drinking like that!" Josh said, and Will added, "Why don't you give me that."

Jordie turned to him, and for a moment there was a murderous rage in his eyes. Then he handed the pint to Will and grinned. "Plenty more where that came from."

Will slipped the pint into his own pocket. He asked quietly, "Are you still taking your pills, Jordie?"

"Just like on the list," Jordie answered, a bit slurrily. "Always follow the list."

"Isn't it a bad idea to drink so much while you're on your meds?"

Jordie swung his head around, and again that murderous glow came into his eyes. "Don't tell me what to do."

Tamping a touch of fear that crawled up his back, Will kept his voice level. "I'm just thinking about you, bud—"

"Well, don't." He waved his hand, his anger gone. "Got a list..."

"What kind of list—"

"Here we are!" Josh interrupted, pulling with a braking squeal into Jordie's driveway. He pushed open his door and gave Will a look that said, "Not now."

They unloaded everything into the house, first setting up the folding table in Jordie's immaculately cleaned room and then arranging the amp and other equipment. The records came next, and while Will and Josh carried the last of the milk crates in, Jordie was meticulously lining up everything.

"Jeez," Josh said, trying to sound cheerful, "when did you learn to make a bed?"

Jordie looked up quickly. "It was on the list. I do everything that's on the list."

Will was about to open his mouth but Josh shot him another look that told him to hold off.

"Guess we should get going," Josh said.

Jordie was inspecting his mixer, pushing it into line with the amp. He nodded without looking up.

"See you around," Josh added. "You said your mom and Aunt will be back in a few days?"

Jordie nodded again, reaching into his still unzipped jacket to pull out yet another pint bottle of Scotch, this one unopened. He twisted the metal cap off with a snap and swallowed some of it.

In the cab of Josh's truck, Will said, "Can I talk now?"

"You're right, he's completely fucked up," Josh said. "Every room looked like it had been scrubbed by a Navy swabbie. And he's drinking way too much. We have to keep an eye on him."

In his room, Jordie heard the roar of Josh's truck peeling out of his driveway, and then up the street. He was finished with the equipment, everything was lined up perfectly, like the list said.

He pulled the list from his pocket, opening it carefully on a clear spot on his DJ table, and smoothed it out. It was a long list now, and growing.

He fished a pen, which he now always carried with him, out of his pocket. He paused, as if listening to something only he could hear.

After consideration, he nodded, and added to the bottom of the list: KILL WILL AND JOSH.

Chapter 9

Annabeth Turner stood before a large, heavy-looking wooden door painted a dark shade of orange. The door curved up into a half-circle at the top. Inset into this section was a stained glass inset in the shape of a pumpkin. The glass had been stained the same color as the door.

The stained-glass section was too high to try to look into, so she rang the bell.

The house the door was attached to, which was at 1420 Acre Street, was a low, squatting, gloomy affair. Though it was just off Main Street, it looked as if it had shrunk away from the larger community of houses. It was surrounded by trees on all sides which seemed to press in on it. Unraked leaves of dark golden red and brown and yellow had washed like ocean drifts against the foundation of the house and a tall pine, in its entirety, had fallen over, victim to some storm or fierce wind, and lay on the right side of the house, with its root system, now dried as a knot of branches, pointing at the front walk. Though it was daylight, and the last day of Pumpkin Days, with noise and laughter and bright October Saturday sunshine behind her on Main Street, Annabeth felt as if she had walked into a gloomy forest.

She rang the bell again, and this time heard a deep *Bong, Bong* echo far within the house.

There was the sound of shuffling, slippered feet approaching the door, which seemed to go on for much too long a time.

Finally they stopped, without seeming to get any louder.

She saw a shadow pass across the stained glass pumpkin.

The door made an unnaturally loud creaking sound as it opened a wide crack, giving her a view of an old wrinkled face, like the face of a capuchin monkey, attached to a thin, robed body not much taller than her own.

"Yes?"

A shadow seemed to pass across the whole world; she glanced up and saw, barely, through the dark tree tops that a huge white cloud had crossed the sun.

The voice was strong and deep but papery. The eyes, behind spectacles as thick as pats of butter, were

large but rheumy, extremely light blue, a blue that was almost white. A fall of long wispy white hair fell from high on his forehead back over the rear of his skull, which was almost orange.

"Are you T. R. Reynolds?" Annabeth asked, in as strong a voice as she could muster.

The wizened monkey's head broke into a smile. "You must have read my book," he said. "No one calls me T.R. but my publisher, who is me, of course."

The door opened wider and now Annabeth smelled Vicks Vapo Rub, and another, drier smell, like old books. Reynolds, she now saw, was indeed shod in slippers, which looked to be of old cracked black leather; there was a golden fringe around the foot opening. The visible portion of his foot between slipper and the bottom of his cuffed flannel pajamas was blue-veined and delicate-looking.

Annabeth thought that if she blew on the man, he might break into dust motes.

"And you are?" Reynolds asked, his voice still showing pleasure; he had thankfully stopped grinning, which had showed her a mouth of dentures backed by few other teeth, and red inflamed gums.

"My name is Annabeth Turner," she answered, in the serious voice she had practiced all morning. "Yes, I read your book and loved it. I'd like to talk to you about Volume Two—"

"Ah!" Reynolds said, in a stronger, suddenly sad voice. "In that case, you'll have to come in..."

The door opened wider, making an even louder creak which Annabeth was sure would bring someone running from Main Street. But as she stepped into the now-wide opening the outside world, sounds and light, seemed chopped off as if with an axe.

The door closed behind her, leaving her in almost total darkness except for a faint amber cast through the pumpkin stained-glass in the door.

By its light she saw a low wooden stool behind the door, against the wall — Reynolds must have used it to step up and look out at her through the pumpkin window.

Reynolds was already shuffling off down a hallway. His slippers made a much louder, more annoying sound here inside the house. As he passed a doorway he flicked a switch on the hallway wall and a flare of illumination burst from within a room behind the opening; now Annabeth, behind him, could make out art objects in the hallway — a dark wooden chest in the shape of a squatting beast, with its head hinged open at the cranium to reveal a red felt-lined cavity within. On the walls were dark paintings, mostly forest scenes; there was a sconce in the shape of a pumpkin without a top, unlit.

"Come into the parlor, Ms. Turner!" Reynolds rasped heartily. She caught up to him only to see him disappear into the back of a room even gloomier than the hallway — deeply dark red damask chairs and, behind an ebony coffee table, a Sheridan sofa that almost looked to be clad in black velvet. The only illumination in the room came from a single lamp next to one of the damask chairs, which she quickly sat down in.

Reynolds was fussing over a dark fireplace against the far wall, leaning down and poking at it with a long twig; she realized he was trying to light a fire within with a long match. The mantle above the fireplace was lined with what looked like tiny taxidermied animals — a field mouse, a chipmunk, a red squirrel in a fiendish pose, on its hind legs with its front claws ready for a fight, mouth opened in a silent hiss.

Reynolds threw the match down in disgust and turned around. "Is it all right if we don't have a fire, Ms. Turner?"

"It's warm enough in here," Annabeth answered.

It was — it was as dry and airless as the inside of a toaster.

"Very well." He shuffled to the black sofa, and settled himself in the middle of it. It seemed to swallow him up for a moment, until he came to rest and sat with his hands folded.

"What, then, would you like to know about Volume Two of my book?"

Annabeth replied, "Will it be out soon?"

There was a long moment of silence, during which Annabeth heard the whisper of a ticking clock somewhere else, faraway in the depths of the house.

"It will never be out," T.R. Reynolds finally replied.

"Why not?"

The pause was longer this time; and Annabeth distinctly heard the faraway striking of a chime for four o'clock.

"Because I want to live."

Annabeth was about to speak when Reynolds spoke again. "You see, Ms. Turner, the legend about Samhaim is true."

"I know. I've...spoken to him."

"So have I, Ms. Turner." His eyes behind his spectacles seemed to have faded entirely to white. "In a pumpkin field, last October, he appeared to me and asked me politely — a voice in my head, not unkind but with what I would call an undercurrent of authority — not to publish the second volume of my book. At that time I had finished writing it, and had only to satisfy my own curiosity regarding the existence of Samhain. He had no problem with the first volume, he even complimented me on it, but did not want the second part to be published. 'A special request,' he called it."

He leaned closer, looking slightly to the side of where Annabeth was sitting, before focusing on her again. "I don't see very well these days, I'm afraid.

And my health, as you can see, is precarious. However..."

He rose from the black couch unsteadily, and shuffled off to a large chest on the wall behind him. Above the chest was yet another dark painting of a landscape: a tiny house, lit from within, surrounded by mountains and a brooding sky.

He drew the top drawer of the chest open. It slid out with the screech of dried wood. He took something out, long and bulky, and shuffled back to the sofa. He placed what he held — a large, thick dun-colored folder — on the ebony coffee table.

He sat back, the sofa swallowing even more of him.

"There it is, Ms. Turner. He told me to give it to you when you came."

Annabeth sat stunned, and then reached for the folder, drawing it into her lap.

Reynolds was studying her closely. "The thing I don't understand — one against many things, I'm afraid — is why he chose you instead of me. But he became quite peevish when I asked that question."

Annabeth said nothing.

"Quite peevish. You might study the copyright page on this second volume, Ms. Turner. It will prove instructive. And I won't counsel you to be careful, because you already haven't been. Perhaps some day my son, who is in California with his mother at the moment, will return and continue my work. Please do show yourself out."

As Annabeth got up, clutching the folder, she again smelled the odor of Vicks, and saw that T.R. Reynolds was crying. She stood watching him. He turned his wizened face away from her, and lifted his paper-thin, blue-veined hands to cover his face.

"Please go."

She quickly left the room, the hallway, the house, hearing the monstrously loud creak of the front door slamming behind her.

At the street, as if a switch had been thrown, the day was still bright, blue-skied, chilly-warm with early autumn. She looked back, and Reynolds' house looked even darker, lost in its night trees.

She hurried home, enjoying the late warmth of the day.

In her room, sitting at her desk, she drew out the mass of paper, which had already been printed as proof pages, awaiting only corrections and return to the printer. She paged quickly past the title page, feeling a thrill at the words VOLUME TWO, 1941-THE PRESENT, and scanned the copyright page. It looked similar to that of the first volume: the date of (proposed) publication, ISBN number, copyright information, author information for library cataloging purposes —

Her eyes locked on the author information, which she had, indeed, looked over in the first volume but which had not come back to strike her as odd today.

The date of birth for T.R. Reynolds was listed, making him only twenty-eight years old.

Chapter 10

I still have my doubts.

The girl will be fine. The two men I am already sure of.

I've told you before, this way is the trickiest. There are other ways.

But none as direct.

You've failed with this before—

1941 was an experiment. I learned from it.

And 1981?

A failure, I admit. But I learned from that, too. It is the unpredictability of these creatures that astounds me. It always has. You assume you know them—

One would think that Death would know them well.

One would think that the opposite of creation would know them better, Dark One. Death is only part of what they are. Sometimes they almost interest me.

As long as you say 'almost.' When they truly start to interest you I will wonder about you. It is still the girl I have questions about.

As I said, she will be fine. All will be fine. And, as I said, we have insurance. My time of the year is coming, and all will be ready.

I hope so, my friend. For your sake.

Chapter 11

The Pumpkin Tender was in desolation.

It had begun to rain the day after the end of Pumpkin Days, and it continued to rain for four days after that. Cold, damp rain, the precursor to winter snow, a slate gray sky, the ground sodden with water. His fields, empty as they were, had gone quickly to ruin, furrows filling with mud, some turning to shallow lakes of brown water. The pumpkins in his special field had begun to rot; normally he would have built a shelter for them, tended them until well past Thanksgiving, ensuring that the few that remained planted in the ground were nourished, their stalks bright green as long as possible before coming Winter. Now they lay, picked and unpicked alike, in a sodden mess, the ripest of them rotting from within, bursting along their seams, ruined, smelling of decay.

For three days he had waited for the large pumpkin with two lobes to speak to him again, huddled beneath his wet blanket, shivering, eyes glued to the fruit — but nothing had happened. Finally, when he ventured close enough to inspect it, he saw that its stem had dropped away from its top, and worms were crawling into the soggy opening, feasting on the grayish-yellow pulp within.

After that he moved farther away from his fields, limping up into the low hills surrounding Orange-field, where no one could find him.

There was a cave set into one of the hills, and he spent one night in it until what looked like a wolf, but might have been a feral dog, chased him out, teeth bared, growling. After that there was nowhere completely dry for him to stay, and after a second night under the rain his skin was as wrinkled as a prune, splotched purple.

He was afraid of his own dreams, and slept little.

He ate nothing for the first day, but then, his stomach screaming with hunger, he foraged for roots and whatever else looked edible. In this he made one great mistake, and spent one entire night groaning in a squat, his sodden pants around his ankles, as his bowels sought to tear themselves from his body.

The next morning he awoke, after barely an hour of sleep, shivering and with fever. His leg ached like fire.

It was then that the wolf, or feral dog, tracked him and began to circle as he lay on the ground.

He prayed that the beast might attack him, and tear out his throat, and be done with it. Everything would be over then. All the dreams, the bad memories, the shattered bits of his life, everything he didn't want put together again.

He actually fell asleep, in the rain, and waited, almost soothed, for the worst.

But nothing happened, and when he woke up the rain had stopped, and the cold clouds were pulling away. Behind them was a measure of blue sky, and then the sun came back and the temperature rose.

He was almost dry, covered in his Army blanket, which had, miraculously, become dry itself. He no longer trembled, and his fever was gone.

His leg was free of pain.

He sat up on dry ground, on a little rise which fell away to dry woods in front and in back of him.

The dog which had followed him was a few yards away, torn to shreds, its own throat ripped open, its mouth open, teeth bared, in a silent cry of agony.

The Pumpkin Tender began to rock back and forth, making weeping sounds.

There, there, the voice in his head came, *didn't I tell you everything would be all right?*

His rocking became more frantic, his mewling sounds more frightened.

The thing in the black cape melted out of the woods in front of him. In sunlight, there was still no face visible, only a dark, shaped void beneath the cowl. There was no physical form visible beneath the folds of the garment — it was as if the garment itself was the creature.

Aaron, the thing said, in a soothing voice, *if I'd known you'd be so upset by what I told you, I never would have said it. Do you think I want to hurt you? I only want to help you. I thought remembering would help you.*

The Pumpkin Tender continued to rock, shaking his head violently.

Do you believe I want to help you?

Again Aaron shook his head violently.

How can I prove it to you? Would you like to forget again?

Now the Pumpkin Tender nodded, making a choking noise. He tried closing his eyes but the image of the caped thing was still there, as if his lids didn't exist. He made a louder choked crying sound.

The shape advanced on him. Suddenly it put its hand, a black, shapeless thing, on Aaron's head. It was colder than ice. A feeling more numbing than any he had ever felt went down through Aaron's head along his back, spreading like expanding cracks in a frozen pond.

I can let you forget again, Aaron, the shape whispered. *I can take the memories away from you.*

Frantically, he nodded, in fear and need.

But tell me first: do the memories hurt you?

A quick nod.

Do they make you want to hurt yourself?

Another nod.

Do they?

He cried out, yanking his head away from the creature's touch, and fell shivering to the ground. Over and over he mouthed in silent agony the word, "Yes..."

Good, then. Remember them one more time, and I will take them from you...

The creature's hand reached out, impossibly long, and its hand once more rested on the Pumpkin Tender's head...

He wasn't the Pumpkin Tender, or Frankenstein. He was Aaron Peters, Private First Class, and he had a letter in his pocket from his sweetheart. Peggy hadn't written in a week, and he was afraid the mail had been held up, or censored out of existence, or maybe in the crashed C-47 cargo plane that had gone down ten days before after being hit by a rebel rocket.

But now he finally had a letter from her in his breast pocket, next to his heart, and the world was right again.

"Hey, dogshit, you gonna read that thing or what?" Kip Berger kidded him. They had gone out on a reconnaissance sweep an hour ago, just after mail call, the two of them on the ground with a truck fifty yards behind.

Aaron grinned and patted his heart. "Got it right here, numb-nuts. I always put her letters here before I do the day's work. Keeps me safe."

"She must be one helluva bang."

Aaron's grin disappeared, and he turned to Berger, balling his fists. "I'd take that back—"

But Berger's big smile calmed him down. "I'm just jealous, is all. I've been married to my fist so long, it makes me crazy when I see a guy with a real girl waiting for him."

Aaron relaxed. For the next five minutes they walked on silently, inspecting the bushes in front of them, the dry horizon ahead of them.

Finally Berger, who couldn't be quiet for long, said, "I hate this job. The shitheads with the mine-sweepers go through ahead of us, and then we get to hope they did their fucking job and cleared out all the fragmentation stake mines, the Claymores—"

"You know how it is — some of these bastards are homemade, or minimum metal jobs, and don't have enough metal parts for the clearance robots or detectors to pick them up. You can thank the Russians for selling to these warlord assholes."

"Yeah, well, I still think it sucks—"

Suddenly Berger stopped dead. His face went white. "Hey, Aaron—"

Aaron stood still, and looked to where Berger was pointing: at his right boot, frozen in place.

Berger said in a measured voice, "I think I just stepped on one of the fuckers we were just talking about, bud."

"Don't move."

"No shit."

Aaron studied the ground around Berger's boot, looking for another slight depression or suspicious turn in the soil.

"Looks like there's only one," Aaron said. "No trip wire, or your leg would be gone by now. It's a wooden plate. It'll go off if you lift your foot."

"That's the good news, right?"

"There's only good news today, Kip."

"Tell it to the Marines. My foot is starting to fall asleep."

"Just hang on, pal."

Berger managed a faint smile, and pointed to his crotch. "Hang onto this."

"I'll get the C.O."

"Well hurry it up, then!" Berger's voice had taken on a note of urgency.

Aaron quickly covered the ground they had cleared, breaking into a trot. The C.O.'s truck was stopped fifty yards back, and he reached it, saluted, and reported what had happened.

"Shit," the C.O., a small, swarthy man with a two-day stubble and tired eyes, said. "It sounds homemade, and it's probably got a big charge in it. Last time we tried to move a weight over one of those mines to transfer the pressure, it still blew. Cut the poor bastard in half."

"Is there something else we can do?"

The C.O. shook his head. "S.O.P., Peters, which means they haven't come up with anything better. I know they tried just about everything else you could think of — foam, debris containment, you name it. Weight transfer is still the only thing that might work."

He gave an order, and the sergeant sitting next to him jumped out and went to the back of the truck. Aaron followed him.

"How much does Berger weigh?" the Sergeant asked.

"I'd say about one-seventy. Maybe one-seventy-five."

The sergeant pulled a box out and began to fill it with measured weights. "That means we need about sixty pounds. You think you can handle this alone?"

"Sure."

The sergeant finished with the box, closed and latched it, and handed it to Peters, along with three five-foot sections of metal pole. He explained exactly what had to be done.

"Tell the poor bastard we're praying for him."

"Right."

Aaron lugged the box back to Berger, and set it on the ground with a grunt.

"You weigh about one-seventy, right?"

"One eighty-five."

"Shit."

Berger looked at him, the strain evident on his features. "Whatever you've got in the box, use it. I can't wait too much longer. There are pins and needles up and down my leg, and I can't feel it anymore."

"Okay." Aaron shuffled the box along the ground toward Berger's frozen foot, stopping about six inches away.

"You ready?"

"No."

"What's the matter?"

Berger looked at him with frightened eyes. "What the hell do you mean, *what's the matter?* I'm scared shitless! And don't tell me this works every time, because I know it hardly ever works. I was at the same briefing you were. I was sitting right next to you when they said say goodbye to your ass if you get in this jam."

To his embarrassment, Aaron noticed that Berger had wet himself.

"Maybe they were wrong." Aaron was fitting the first section of the pole to a catch on the box; then he would fit subsequent sections into the rear of the one in front of it, until he was fifteen feet away. Then he would push the box forward to replace Berger's weight on the mine. "You set?"

"Not yet, bud. I want you to do me a big favor."

Peters snapped the last section of pole into place. He looked up quizzically.

Berger said, "I want you to read me that letter from your girl."

Aaron straightened. "Jeez."

Berger pleaded, "Please, bud. For luck. Maybe some of the luck you always get will fall on me."

"You got it." Aaron put down the pole and pulled the letter out from its place near his heart. He ripped open one edge and pulled the single sheet out, waiting for the whiff of perfume that always accompanied Peggy's letters to him.

There was no perfume.

He flipped open the letter.

"Read it," Berger demanded. "Out loud."

Aaron was scanning the letter, his eyes starting at the signature on the bottom, which read *Yours sincerely*, instead of *All my love*, to the top, which started: *Dear Aaron, things have happened in the last few weeks...*

"Read it, dammit!" Berger begged.

The world drew away from Aaron Peters; suddenly he didn't see the dusty road, or Berger, or the thin blue sky of Mogadishu, or anything. A hissing came into his head, and the spot next to his heart where the letter had been began to burn as if it was on fire. His hand holding the letter dropped to his side, and the words *no longer*, and *wish you well in the future* drained out of him as if a stopcock had been opened on his life. He was suddenly dry, and light as air. The letter floated to earth. He was standing next to Berger, but didn't see him, or hear his shouting voice.

Then suddenly he did. "*What the hell – !*" he heard as he put his hands on Berger and pushed, and slid his boots forward to replace himself on the mine, which then went off.

He heard the explosion from far away, and saw Berger cut into pieces in front of him, as if drawn and quartered in mid-air — the bottom parts, which had been his legs and thighs, suddenly red, flying one way while the top parts, bloody as well, a severed arm, and the rest of the torso, with something heaving in the open chest and with the other arm still reaching for him and the face still asking "*What the hell*" flew impossibly the other way. And then as Berger receded everything faded from his face, all emotion and questions, and he turned white and dead. And then there was a burn up Aaron's own leg and sound came back in a rush like a turned-up volume knob and he heard that tearing sound, of meat being ripped off a bone, his own meat and Berger's, and then another louder sound of all the screams, his own impossibly high screams until something slammed into his chin and up through his mouth....

The impossibly cold hand on the Pumpkin Tender's head slid away in a retreating caress.

Suddenly the memories were gone.

All of them.

He was the Pumpkin Tender, and Frankenstein.

But he was no longer Aaron Peters, Private First Class, who had murdered his buddy and tried, unsuccessfully, to murder himself.

He was nothing now, only a mess of a former man — a man who remembered little if anything and took care of pumpkins.

Didn't I tell you I'd take care of you? Haven't I always taken care of you?

The touch of the freezing hand came back, and with it one more memory, which flared briefly in his head before dissipating like smoke:

When he came back from Somalia, and after all the time in the V.A. hospital, and then the discharge, an honorable one because the administration didn't want any more blots on the Somalia campaign, especially not after losing all those men, and those helicopters, when they went after that warlord — after all that time, there was nothing wrong with his memory. He could remember what he had done perfectly. He had begun to limp around Orangefield, keeping his horrible secret to himself, from his family, from his friends, because he couldn't live with it.

And he had decided not to live with it.

So one night the first October after he returned, when the moon looked Halloween orange as it rose off the horizon and it was cold, he had gone out to one of the empty pumpkin fields on the outskirts of Orangefield, a field owned by a man named Froelich, and he had stood in that almost empty, almost picked-clean pumpkin field, smelling rotting sweet pumpkin carcasses around him, facing the moon, and he had put his service revolver to his head.

Only, something had risen out of that field in front of him, something like a black cape which blotted the moon from view, and he had lowered the service revolver while the thing made promises.

You already belong to me, the thing said, reasonably. *You should have died in Somalia, the way you intended, so you are already mine. You're living on borrowed time, and in agony, but I will protect you. I will make you forget. Isn't forgetfulness what you really want, Aaron? Isn't that why you came out here tonight — to forget?*

He nodded, dropping the gun. He began to weep, and tried to talk with his ruined mouth: "I... k-k-killed —"

Yes, Aaron. But I'll help you to forget, until it's time for you to help me. Do you understand?

Aaron was weeping. "I...ki...illed..."

And then the freezing had first fallen on his head, and with it blessed forgetfulness.

And then, suddenly, he understood what he could do, what loving service he could perform, and he had become, then and now, the Pumpkin Tender.

Chapter 12

Kathy Marks could not stop thinking about Annabeth Turner.

What is it about her?

Ever since Annabeth had taken three restricted books from the library — returning them the next day while Kathy was not on duty, which the librarian was sure had been deliberate — Kathy had felt a strange affinity for the girl, something that went beyond the tug of outsider recognition she had felt for Annabeth initially.

Is it because she lost her father, and I lost my parents?

A brief memory of Aunt Jane and Uncle Ed, who'd taken Kathy in after the car accident, rose into her consciousness, and she shivered.

Or am I afraid for her because of what happened to me afterwards?

Annabeth and her mother had moved to Orangefield, the librarian knew, at the beginning of the summer. Mr. Turner had died the year before. Kathy had deduced that things were not good at home — that Annabeth's mother, in the girl's phrase, had "problems." There had also been the hint of social services involvement, which could mean anything from child neglect to outright abuse. Kathy had driven by the house one evening after work and found it unkempt and lonely-looking — the poor relation on a block of neatly trimmed cape houses.

Why am I so worried about her?

Without really knowing why, she suddenly decided that tonight she would stop by the house and see the girl.

There was something sad and desperate about her, something that reminded her of herself at that age.

And something else that she couldn't put her finger on, something to do with the voice she had heard in the library that night...

The library was busy, for a Tuesday night, and she was occupied until just before 9:00. And then, suddenly, she was alone. Her student assistant Paul, after turning out most of the lights, was through the door at the stroke of the hour, and with the bang of the closing, locked door Kathy found herself with a little paperwork and a silent library.

The wind had picked up at the windows, making the sound that always reminded her of moaning.

And now there was another sound which drowned out the moan.

It was the voice she had heard the night Annabeth had taken the three restricted books.

Kathy.

Again, as it had that night, the vaguest of dark memories tried to rise, then melted away. She felt herself go cold all over.

Kathy. Speak to me.

The voice had moved to one of the other windows, and then she heard it from the darkened back of the library.

Kathy.

She heard the shuffle of steps in one of the aisles, the sound of books being moved aside.

Call me Sam...

The librarian marched to the bank of lights by the front door, threw on the florescents in the back of the library.

She felt something cold touch her finger, brush up her left arm and across her neck. There was a whisper in her ear.

It's me. Sam...

The windows began to rattle — all of them at once, a sound as if they would all shatter to bits.

The suspended overhead florescent lights began to sway.

Kathy ran to her desk, grabbed for her purse and jacket.

A stack of books, waiting to be checked in, flew off the desk in three directions.

Kathy.

She ran for the door and the newspaper rack came alive as she passed, magazines and the daily newspapers flying up like flapping birds at her.

She covered her face and cried out as newspapers hit her in the face, magazines slapped at her legs.

Annabeth is mine.

The voice was all around her, whispering in her ear and shouting at her from the back of the library simultaneously.

The window rattling rose to a breaking point—

And then stopped.

The library was silent.

The overhead hanging lights swayed to a squeaking halt.

The newspapers fluttered to the floor around her.

Kathy Marks stood by the doorway, panting, eyes wide.

She let out a single, frightened sob.

In her car, she regained her composure. She sat steadying her breath, watching the darkened library building in front of her. The lights were out, the building quiet.

Whoever you are, she thought, *you won't stop me.*

As she pulled away, once more determined to visit Annabeth Turner, the lights in the library, unseen to her, blinked on for a moment, and something dark passed before the front windows.

The house was even untidier and sadder-looking than she remembered. There were empty garbage cans at the curb that needed taking in. The grass needed mowing and the flower beds to either side of the front door were choked with dry weeds.

The paint on the shutters was peeling, and the front steps groaned with rotted wood when she stepped on them.

She rang the doorbell three times, hearing nothing, and then knocked loudly on the door.

She still heard nothing.

Daring herself, she walked around to the side of the house, almost stepping on a rusted rake left carelessly, tines up.

The first floor windows along the front were all dark, but she detected the glow of faint light in a window on the second floor of the house.

She walked to the back of the house, which was even more overgrown, and looked up — there was a light on in the single second story window.

She went back to the front door and banged on it repeatedly.

She heard a rustle of movement inside the house, followed by a grunt.

She banged again.

She heard more movement, a slurred voice: "Whozzit?"

"Mrs. Turner," she called, "it's Kathy Marks, from the Orangefield Library. May I speak with you, please?"

There was a groan, and then silence.

Kathy banged on the door again. "Mrs. Turner, I need to talk with you about Annabeth!"

Another groan from within, and then a sound as if someone had fallen to the floor. She heard a curse, and then slow, measured steps from behind the door.

The door was yanked open, and a blowzy, angry face appeared.

"What the hell you want?"

The door was thrown all the way open, and the woman, who was dressed in a dirty housecoat and slippers, nearly lurched at her. The librarian was forced to step back by the strong sour smell of gin.

Behind her the house was filthy, cluttered and dark, all the way back to the second-story stairway and the kitchen beyond, where a cat crouched, staring at her suspiciously.

"Mrs. Turner—"

"I said what the hell you want! Botherin' me at all hours! What'd she do? What'd the brat do?"

Kathy took a breath before answering reasonably: "Annabeth didn't do anything, Mrs. Turner. I'm here because I'm concerned about her—"

"Concerned about wha'? Get out! Leave me alone! I ain't a bad parent. I can do what has to be done! No goddam social services bitch is gonna tell me otherwise!"

"I'm not from social services, Mrs. Turner—"

"Dammit! Leave us alone! Leave us all alone!"

Behind Mrs. Turner Kathy saw Annabeth slowly descending the stairs and staring at her intently. She stopped at the bottom.

The librarian took a step forward and tried to reason directly with the girl. "Annabeth, can I speak with you please?"

"I brought the books back," the girl said defensively.

"It's not about that—"

Mrs. Turner suddenly lunged forward, holding on to Kathy Marks and breathing directly in her face. Kathy saw Annabeth run back up the stairs.

"It ain't right! Get out! Get out!"

Kathy moved back, disengaging herself from Mrs. Turner.

"I'm sorry I bothered you, Mrs. Turner."

"An' don't come back!" Mrs. Turner shouted, slamming the door shut.

The librarian stood staring at the front door for a moment.

I told you she's mine.

It was the voice again, from the library.

Annabeth belongs to me, Kathy.

A swirl of pure cold rose up around her, like a tornado, driving her from the front walk.

Mine.

Kathy Marks turned and ran for her car, opening the door and slamming it behind her.

The dervish of wind was left in the street, where it circled down to nothingness.

Kathy Marks drove slowly away, stopping once, without really knowing why, still breathing hard and trembling, to look back at the second floor of the house.

Chapter 13

"Dude!"

As Josh got out of the cab of his black Ford truck, Jordie nearly rushed forward to hug him. Josh took a step back, hesitating, but Jordie seemed to be in such a good mood that he gave a short laugh and allowed himself to be nearly picked up off the ground.

Jordie dropped him, looked around him into the truck's cab.

"Hey, where's Will?"

"Couldn't come," Josh answered. "Had to do some stuff for his mom."

"Mom. Yeah, cool."

Josh looked into his friend's face, and saw that the pupils were as wide as dimes.

Shit, hammered again, he thought.

"Maybe I should come back later, Jordie," he said. He hitched a thumb at the cab. "Truck needs an oil change—"

"Hell, I'll *buy* you an oil change, after we move that shit I told you about. We'll go over to the Jiffy Lube, then pick up Will—"

"I don't think Will can make it at all today," Josh said.

"No shit?" A dark cloud passed over Jordie's face, and Josh thought he heard him mumble, "Not on the list, man..."

"List?"

Jordie seemed to touch earth again. "Shit, man — just you and me, then! Dynamic duo, just like fifth grade!"

Josh was suddenly uncomfortable. He looked past Jordie at the house. The rest of the driveway was uncluttered by cars, and the open garage was empty. "Your mom and Aunt ever get home?"

"Huh? Sure! Days ago. They went out for lunch or something. You know how these modern couples are..." He laughed, and leaned closer. "Hey, wanna get stoned?" he whispered.

The inside of the house looked as spotless as the last time he'd been in it. In fact, it looked *exactly* like the last time he'd been in it, more than a week and a half ago. There wasn't even a cereal box out of place in the kitchen. More out of curiosity than hunger, he opened the refrigerator and said, "Got anything to eat—"

The fridge was completely empty, not even an egg in its plastic nest — no milk, no butter, no fruit in their bins, no cottage cheese—

A weird chill went up Josh's back.

"Jeez, Jordie, what the hell have you been living on?"

When he turned around Jordie was right in front of him, grinning as he pushed something long and bright into Josh's stomach.

"Sorry, man," Jordie whispered, "but it's on the list."

Josh opened his mouth wide to speak, but Jordie shook his head and ripped the blade viciously up through his middle.

A bright blurt of blood formed in Josh's open mouth, and then his eyes clouded over and he became a weight against the open refrigerator, which began to hum.

Jordie let him down easily to the floor, then pushed him aside with his booted foot and closed the refrigerator door.

"Have to clean that again, man," he said, focusing on the drops of red splattered on the door.

Find Will, the voice in his head told him.

Forty minutes later, after bringing Josh's body to the cellar and lining it up neatly with that of his mother and aunt, which were already limed and tarped, he climbed into the cab of Josh's truck and pulled it out onto the road. The day was bone chilly, but he wore only his light jacket over a tee-shirt and jeans. In the flatbed was his d.j. equipment, carefully wrapped and tied down. On the seat next to him in the cab was an open piece of paper with Will's name on it, and a pile of pill bottles. On the bottom of the list, after Will's name, was the phrase, *Take your meds, in the proportions I told you.*

Will's house was empty, which started to panic him, but the voice in his head calmed him down, telling him to take one Zyprexa, which he did dry, because he had forgotten to take any Scotch with him.

I didn't want you to take any Scotch, the voice said, and he said out loud, "Oh, yeah," and remembered one of the other things on the list.

And drive slowly, the voice added.

He slowed the truck down to thirty as he came into town, matching the speed limit.

It was a busy Thursday afternoon, and the business district of Orangefield was crowded with traffic. Most of the parking spots along Main were taken, and the bank parking lot was full. He spotted

Will's mother's Malibu in one of the bank slots near the front.

Park across the street.

He circled around the block again, coming back out on Main Street behind the bank, and pulled into a street spot across from the bank as someone pulled out ahead of him.

Check the meter.

He got out of the car, and saw that there was twenty minutes left on the parking meter.

Put a quarter in.

He started to protest, then stopped when a woman walking a baby stroller looked at him oddly.

Do it.

He fished a quarter out of his pocket, noting that it was a Delaware commemorative — hadn't his aunt collected those? Did she have this one? Maybe he should save it for her — and then remembered that she was dead and didn't collect them any more. He slid the quarter into the meter slot.

Get back in the cab and wait for them to come out. Then follow them.

He did so, and turned on the radio — he turned the dial away from Josh's alternative rock station and zeroed in on the rap station he listened to. He cranked up the volume —

Turn it down.

"But—"

The voice was less pleasant: *Now.*

121

He shrugged and turned down the volume so that it couldn't be heard on the street.

After a half-hour of music mixed with what seemed like a hundred commercials (*Got to find another station to listen to*, he thought) he was reaching for the dial when the voice said: *Look.*

He looked up and saw Will and his mother, a petite brunette with a no-nonsense look on her face, leaving the bank and heading for their car.

Follow.

Jordie turned on the engine and pulled out behind Will's car.

Back a little. So they don't see you.

He let another car pull out from the curb in front of him, and kept himself a discrete distance behind that.

There were two more stops — the pharmacy, which Will's mother ran into while Will stayed behind the wheel, and then the supermarket.

Jordie groaned as Will and his mother parked and headed into the food store with a cart.

Be patient. Listen to the radio again. Take a Clozaril.

Jordie kept the radio on while he rummaged through the pile of pill bottles, drawing one oblong pill out and, again, swallowing it dry.

"Damn! I need some Scotch for that!" He eyed the liquor store next to the supermarket but the voice said:

No.

Anger flared up but the pill kicked in quickly, calming him. He lazily spun the tuner on the radio, looking for a more commercial-free rap station, but it wasn't to be found.

"How long are we going to have to—"

There. They're coming out. Follow them like before.

"James Bond," Jordie laughed, bringing the truck's engine to life again.

He kept a distance from Will's car, and was rewarded when it headed straight out of town.

In a few minutes it had pulled off the main road into Will's neighborhood, and into his driveway, which sided a neat red ranch house with a small porch guarding the white front door.

Wait till they go in the house. Then follow them in and do it.

Jordie held back, parking on the street a few houses away while Will and his mother unloaded the groceries; as Will slammed the car's trunk closed and headed for the house, Jordie pulled up and parked in front of Will's house. As he parked he rummaged beneath the mountain of pill bottles and found the knife he had used on Josh. It still had blood on it.

Get out. Do it.

Jordie climbed out of the truck's cab, hiding the knife in his jacket pocket — he felt something else in there, a bag with some of his marijuana in it.

"Man, sure could use a toke or two now—"

Do it.

He skipped up onto the porch, like he had a thousand times, stepped to the side of the huge pumpkin there, and reached for the doorbell.

He pushed the buzzer twice. As the door opened, revealing Will's surprised mother, a hand clamped on Jordie's arm from behind him as Jordie pulled the knife from his pocket, followed by the bag of marijuana, which fell to the ground —

Jordie twisted around to see the face of deputy sheriff Charley Fredricks.

"*Jeez*," Fredericks said, tightening his grip on the hand with the knife in it. As he did so the knife fell to the ground. "I told you I'd keep an eye on you, Jordie — all I wanted to do was see if you were drunk or stoned!" He yanked both of Jordie's arms behind him while he fished out his cuffs and secured them.

He turned Jordie around. "What the hell were you up to?"

Jordie waited for the voice to give him instructions, tell him what to do or say, but the voice was gone.

He looked the deputy sheriff in the face and grinned. "I was just gonna kill 'em, is all. Just like the others at my house."

PART THREE

Halloween

Chapter 14

The banner had been taken down over City Hall, and the tent was gone from Rainer Park. The grandstand had been dismantled along Main Street. There were no more fireworks, or pumpkin pie eating contests, or parades, or pumpkin rolling contests. The votes for Pumpkin Queen had been tallied, the winner crowned and feted and sent home.

Pumpkin Days were over.

But the orange-painted stripe down the middle of Main Street remained, and so did the lights and the decorations and, of course, the pumpkins.

There was still the matter of Halloween.

October 31st dawned damp and cold, but by nine in the morning the misty rain had dissipated, and blue sky broke through. By eleven the sun had dried the leaves to crisp colors, and the world smelled of apples and burning woodsmoke and candles and pumpkins innards.

As if by magic, the pumpkins of Orangefield, which had gone to bed the night before as faceless fruit, had reappeared in the morning as guardians and monsters. Not real monsters but carved ones, with distinct faces — evil or friendly grins, toothless or toothsome, some with ears, some with triangles for noses, or circles, or rough diamond shapes or no noses at all. There was the work of artists and the work of amateurs and tots.

Orangefield was over-populated by a race of orange faces.

The sun got high but never hot. As the day wore on the sky became bluer, colder; and the wind, a Halloween wind, began to whip the leaves into leaf tornados, and whistle through the pumpkins and make them sing. The store shelves were empty of candy. It was Friday, and after the schools let out for the week there was much unboxing and pinning and cutting as costumes were unpacked or made, sheets became instant ghosts, children grew wax fangs or suddenly became vampires or bats or space invaders. The children of Orangefield disappeared, replaced by one-of-everything-monstrous, waiting for dark.

In the Orangefield Library, Kathy Marks thought of nothing but Annabeth Turner. There was a place in her that turned to ice whenever the image of the tall young girl rose into her mind, and there were roiling memories that tried again and again to climb up from Kathy's forgotten past but refused to become real.

She was sure the girl was in some sort of danger.

She had hoped Annabeth would return to the library to talk to her but it hadn't happened. Kathy had even stopped by the girl's house again, but, this time, no one had come to the door. The librarian had taken to calling the house on the telephone at intervals over the last few days, but to no avail.

For the fourth time that day, she called Annabeth's house, but there was still no answer.

Outside, the wind moaned across the windows. The streets were beginning to fill up with costumed trick-or-treaters.

Soon the trickle would turn into a torrent.

At five o'clock, in a half hour, Kathy would close the library early for the holiday. She had already turned away a few hopeful costumed children, explaining patiently that it was library policy not to serve candy, and that she would be happy to accomodate them when they visited her house later.

Stroking her left forearm lightly with her fingers, she stared at the clock, and then reached once more for the phone.

Chapter 15

Annabeth sat up, blinked and said, "What day is it?"

Don't you know, Wizard? It's our day. It's Halloween.

Halloween?

Could it really be Halloween?

Yes, Wizard, the voice said, soothing. *Finally. The day I show you what I promised. After you do something for me.*

Annabeth stretched, sat up in her desk chair. It felt as if she had been sitting for days. She probably had been. She knew she had stopped going to school, and hadn't eaten much lately, and couldn't remember the last time she'd bathed. She looked down at herself, and couldn't remember the last time she had changed her clothes.

But none of that matters, Wizard. What matters is that you'll see where he is.

"Yes," she said, and suddenly the strange feelings melted away, replaced by a kind of peace. *"I'll see where he is."*

She looked down at the open manuscript pages on her desk, the proof pages of T.R. Reynolds's *Occult Practises in Orangefield and Chicawa County, New York, Volume Two.* The pages she had last turned to were crumpled and stained — she had fallen asleep on them.

But they seemed to glow with truth.

The phone next to her bed rang — she seemed to remember it ringing on and off for some time. She pushed herself away from the desk and reached to answer it.

Don't.

Her hand froze above the phone, and it suddenly stopped ringing.

Almost immediately it began to ring again, and without thinking she snatched the receiver up to her ear.

"Hello?" Her own voice sounded strange, unused.

The voice on the other end sounded frantic. "Annabeth Turner?"

"Yes, but my name now is Wiz—" she began to say.

"This is T.R. Reynolds, Annabeth. I...feel terrible, what I've done to you. I want you to listen to me very carefully. The manuscript I gave you — I want you to destroy it immediately."

"I can't do that."

Reynolds was wheezing, his breath coming in a ragged, uneven rhythm. He tried to speak once but left off in a hacking dusty fit of coughing. "Anna... ...beth..."

"I can't destroy your book," Annabeth said. "It's told me everything I need to know."

"What it's told you is a lie." Reynolds shot out the words, and then lapsed into a long wheezing fight for breath.

Suddenly Annabeth felt her own throat close, as if in sympathy. The voice fighting to speak to her on the other end of the line became very faint. Her vision constricted to a whirl of images and she began to fight for breath—

Asthma attack.

Still clutching the phone with one hand, hearing T.R. Reynolds's strained voice from far away — "...I was...made to write...those...things...there's nothing ...true in...there..." — Annabeth searched frantically with her other hand for her inhaler. It should be in the right-hand pocket of her jeans — but it wasn't there. She dug frantically, clawing at loose change, her house keys, but it was gone.

Still hearing Reynolds's voice — "lies...every-thing lies...he..." — she dug into her other pockets, but came up empty. Her jacket was on the floor next to the desk and she reached frantically down to it, patting its pockets as her breathing became even more ragged, her throat closing — "Anna...beth...are you all...right?" — and suddenly she was on all fours, on the carpet, the phone dropped next to her, trying desperately to pull in air —

—and then her hand fell on the respirator, it must have fallen out of her pocket onto the floor. She yanked it up and put it to her mouth, breathing... breathing...

She rolled over onto her back, as precious oxygen flowed into her lungs again, and her constricted throat began to open.

She closed her eyes and breathed normally, now hearing the phone — a ragged, broken chatter was coming from it. She opened her eyes and saw the receiver nearby, and pulled it to her ear. She got up slowly and sat back at her desk.

"Anna...beth...can you...hear...me...?"

"Yes, Mr. Reynolds, I'm all right."

"I'm...not..." His voice sounded very strained. There was a long pause filled with the same sounds she had just made and then suddenly Reynolds's voice caught and he said, very clearly, "*Oh, God.*"

"Mr. Reynolds?"

"My God, my hands, my hands, *even older —*"

"Mr. Reyn—"

"Annabeth, listen to me!" His voice was rising in pitch, becoming at once more frantic and weaker. "The flesh...is aging before me, on my arms, my hands, *I can see my own bones—*"

There suddenly came a high, unearthly, rasping scream which went on and on and then suddenly stopped.

Annabeth heard what sounded like a pile of something clacking, falling to the floor.

"Mr. Reynolds?" she said, fearfully.

There was hissing silence on the other end of the line.

"Mr. Reynolds?"

He can't hear you, Wizard.

"Oh, no..."

Don't worry about him, Wizard. There are no lies in his book. Hang up the phone.

Slowly, she replaced the phone in its cradle.

"But he—"

We won't think about that. It's not important now. What's important is what you've learned. And what it's going to show you.

"Yes..."

Look at the manuscript again, Wizard.

Annabeth looked down at the open manuscript pages on the desk before her. She smoothed the crumpled edges, pulled at a crease that went through the middle of the left hand page. On it was the chapter title *Eleven: the Bizarre Sightings of 1981.*

For perhaps the hundredth time in the last few days, she began to read:

In 1981 there occurred what remain to this day the strangest Sam sightings of them all. What made them even stranger was their seeming connection to a group of deaths which occurred on and around Halloween of that year.

The first paragraph was ended with an asterisk, which led to a note at the bottom of the page:

(It should be noted before we proceed any further that the police department of Orangefield never considered the deaths of the Halloween season of 1981 to be anything other than coincidence, and no criminal or any other kind of proceedings were ever initiated. As the police chief at the time, Owen Cassidy, stated: "Deaths sometimes cluster at certain times of the year. Because three of these were homicides, with the perpetrator dead himself, I would merely count myself lucky as far as paperwork goes. As for the rest of them, nothing but chance is involved, or maybe the influence of a full moon — or maybe Halloween."

Reynolds then, in the main body of the text, got to the heart of the matter:

Here are the facts as they're known from records: between the first of October, 1981, and the last day of the month, five deaths from unnatural causes were recorded in Orangefield. In the previous year, there had been no homicides, and, indeed, in the previous five years there had been three homicides in toto recorded.

At the same time, during the 1981 Halloween season, there were forty-one separate Sam sightings, up from three the previous year and ten total for the previous five year period. The first deaths, homicides, occurred on October 2nd, when a local pumpkin farmer, Bedel Mayes, hacked his wife and infant son to death with a machete. Mayes had, the week before, reported a Sam sighting in his own field, which was corroborated by his field hand, Derrick Johnson. Johnson himself was killed by Mayes when he discovered the bodies of the first two murder victims in the barn the next day. All three victims were later found laid out in a row, rotting in the same barn; some of the farm's stock, including several pigs which had gotten loose, were reported to have eaten part of the corpses. Mayes then spent the rest of October going about his business and tending his pumpkins, until he killed himself on Halloween. He was found in the barn with his victims. He had attempted to decapitate himself with the same machete he had used on his family and Derrick Johnson. A bizarre phrase (which will be discussed later, see note below) was found carved in the barn's door. There were two other victims with ties to Sam sightings that Halloween. One, Mabel Genes, was a successful suicide who left a short note regarding not only her encounters with Sam, but the promises he had made to her. The other was an attempted suicide, a girl of eleven whose name was protected by the police and her family, but who, according to the local newspaper, the Gazette, had also seen Sam and been influenced by him. She had carved a phrase into her left forearm with the pried-open end of a paperclip, which tied her to the two successful suicides (this phrase will be discussed later; again, see note below) but, after her suicide failed, she apparently had no further contact with Samhain. In fact, according to sources in the police department, the girl remembered nothing of her encounter with Sam or her attempted suicide, and the matter was kept secret. According to one reliable source, she grew up in Orangefield and lives there to this day, unaware of her participation in the events of 1981.

This section ended in another asterisk, which led to another footnote:

(The strange note of Mabel Genes, as well as the phrase from it which tied together the two suicides as well as the attempted suicide, will be discussed in detail in Chapter Fourteen: Who is Sam?)

Annabeth quickly turned ahead to the place she had marked in Chapter Fourteen. She sat staring at a photograph of a middle-aged, slightly dumpy woman with a lopsided smile and kind, moist eyes.

She felt she knew those eyes. The caption under the photograph read: *Mabel Genes.*

Go ahead, Wizard, finish it. Read it again. Read the secret. It's all true.

Annabeth's eyes rested on the well-read section under the photograph; she took a deep breath and read:

And now we come to the strangest item in all the modern canon of Sam sightings, the suicide note of Mabel Genes. By all accounts (and this includes newspaper articles, eye-witness reports, medical records, as well as the testimony of the present author, who knew Ms. Genes and was, in fact, a pupil in her first grade class at Orangefield Elementary at the time) Ms. Genes was gregarious, happy, happily married and well adjusted. Before Halloween of 1981 she showed absolutely no tendency toward depression or self destruction. She was Presbyterian, and devoutly religious.

But something happened in the second week of October of 1981 to change her personality utterly. Her husband said later that she almost appeared obsessed. (As a sidebar, and perhaps an irrelevant or even comical one, it should be remembered that the novel and movie "The Exorcist" had been released within the previous decade.) During that week, after school, Ms. Genes made her annual visit to Froelich Farms to pick pumpkins for her classroom and home. She had been doing this for twenty-two years. While in the field, alone and at the end of the day, she reportedly had an encounter with Samhain — later she told her husband that he had risen up out of the ground like a 'black whirlpool' and spoken to her.

The incident was forgotten, except that Ms. Genes began to have strange dreams (again, as told to her husband) and exhibit increasingly bizarre behavior. This behavior — which included night walking and what appeared to be periodic trances as well as talking when no one was there, abruptly ceased the week before Halloween, just when Mr. Genes was about to schedule her for a doctor's visit. The next week Mrs. Genes, according to her husband and others (including the present author, who had noticed the change in his teacher and then recalled her sudden return to normal — she was known for her wonderful in-class Halloween party, and this party proceeded as planned, two days before the holiday) returned to normal and the matter of medical attention was dropped.

Then, early on the morning of Halloween, which was on a Friday that year, Mabel Genes, was found hanging naked from the family's apple tree in the back yard.

The incident would have faded in memory if not for the bizarre suicide note that was found nailed to the tree. It was not its length (which was brief) but its enigmatic nature that have made it special in the history of Sam literature. For it opens to discussion the entire question of not only who Sam is, but what he represents. The note read, to begin with:

SAM PROMISES LIFE.

If, indeed, Sam is Samhain, the Celtic Lord of Death, what can this part of the note mean? Was Mabel Genes promised, by Samhain, life after death? Would Samhain have this power? If so, who gives it to him? Who does he serve?

There followed a three page discussion of religious and philosophical issues, which Annabeth had read with interest the first time and then discarded as irrelevent. For there was only one more section in the whole volume which held any interest for her. It was the phrase which Sam had drawn her attention to when she first studied the page proofs of *Occult Practises in Orangefield and Chicawa County, New York, Volume Two.*

Annabeth turned to it now.

Do you believe me, Wizard?

Annabeth looked up from the page, looked out the window over her desk down into her backyard, with its own tall elm tree with a sturdy rope ending in a ready noose hanging ready from its strongest limb.

"Yes, I believe you."

Then nothing else matters, does it?

"No."

Good, Wizard. You will do well. And you will get what you want.

"I want to see where he is. Where they all are."

141

It's what I promised Mabel Genes, Wizard. She lost a child which no one, not even her husband, knew about. Just like you lost your father. And you shall see it soon. Read, Wizard. Read the rest of it.

Annabeth looked down at the page proofs:

And now we come to the rest of Mabel Genes's suicide note, and the strangest part of all. For in it she states:
THREE WILL SHOW THE WAY.
These were precisely the words that were found etched by machete into Bedel Mayes's barn door, and the same words the eleven-year-old attempted suicide had carved into her arm with the end of a paperclip.

Annabeth briefly studied her own left forearm, where crusted-over scabs covered the same words she had recently carved there with an open pair of scissors. Then she returned to the page proofs:

It is obvious that 'The Three' refers to the three suicides.
But what will they show the way for?
Or who?

Chapter 16

It won't be long. You should be ready.

I hope so. If I were you I'd still be worried about the girl.

The girl will be no problem. I've told you that.

If not the girl, then interference with her.

It won't happen. And I've turned any possible interference to our advantage.

Was this the 'insurance' you spoke of?

Yes. I'm sure it will work.

You said that the last time. And look what happened.

This time nothing will go wrong. You have only to be prepared.

I hope so — *Sam*. As I said: I worry about the girl.

Even if the girl becomes a problem, there is another ready. As I said: insurance.
Ah....

Chapter 17

The Pumpkin Tender awoke wrapped in his Army blanket, wet, in a furrow in his favorite field. He sat up, and noted that the sky, here in the new morning, was already clearing.

It would be cold and clear later.

His leg ached, and he shivered.

"Do you know what day it is, Aaron?"

He turned to see that the pumpkin with two lobes — now rotting away, the orange furrowed flesh of its face gray and soft — had grown a face again. Its mouth was down-turned, its sad eye holes roiling with worms. Its top had completely caved in.

It turned in its muddy nest with a squishing sound and looked straight at him.

"I said: do you know what day it is, Aaron?"

The Pumpkin Tender said nothing.

The pumpkin's sagging mouth drew up slowly into a smile, bits of rotting fruit and seeds falling from it as it did so.

"It's Halloween, Aaron."

The Pumpkin Tender still said nothing, only drew himself up tighter into his blanket.

"And that means: it's time to remember, Aaron. And forget forever."

Things were so much easier this way. Now that he knew who he was, and knew what he did — and what he had to do — a kind of calm came over him.

If only he had done this a long time ago...

The day had turned beautiful. The morning mist had completely dissipated, leaving the day as cold and clear as any day in October could be. The sky was painfully blue, and the leaves, still clinging to trees or on the ground, were a gift of colors — gold, bright yellow, russet red. The air smelled of leaves and pine and Halloween itself.

He got what he needed from the little space Mr. Froelich let him use in the farm stand's storage shed, and started the long walk to the top of the mountain. His leg felt better than it had in years. On the way he saw Froelich stacking gourds for the tourists who would come after Halloween and into Thanksgiving to fill their city homes with a little of the autumn season.

He used to like Thanksgiving a lot.

Froelich stopped his work when he saw The Pumpkin Tender approach. He stretched his back and put his hands into the pockets of his overalls.

"Aaron! I was beginning to think you disappeared."

The Pumpkin Tender smiled.

"How you feeling these days, son? You did another fine job this year. We'll all look forward to next year."

The Pumpkin Tender continued to smile and limped on.

Froelich pointed at the gunny sack in Aaron's hand. "Going on a little trip?"

The Pumpkin Tender gave a short nod, and kept moving.

"Well, remember, when the weather gets too cold, you come and bed down here, just like always."

Aaron waved.

The long climb went slowly. But he savored every step. He thought of Peggy, and what might have been; and of the days of his childhood, which had been ideal. He had played in these hills every day after school, and hadn't had a care in the world—

Just like now.

He tried to sing out — but only a croak came from his ruined throat.

It would do.

He was no longer Frankenstein.

Or the Pumpkin Tender.

He was just Aaron Peters, who was finally doing what had to be done.

He reached the summit by mid-afternoon. There were no full pumpkin fields to look down on now, no ring of orange fire around Orangefield. In fact, the muddy empty fruit fields that encircled the town would be cold, uninviting places for the rest of the year. But the view was still a good one, the distant town set like a jewel in the midst of wooded hills, and it was still his favorite place.

And today was Halloween.

He opened his gunny sack on the ground and laid out the contents carefully. There was a small picture of Peggy, which he had carried in his wallet when she was his girl. There was a photo of his mother and father, and another of himself the year before he went to Somalia, standing with his brother next to his

Mustang — it was a good color shot, and showed off the car's interior. And there was a photo of Kip Berger in his uniform, helmet tilted back on his head, smiling broadly as if nothing in the world would ever go wrong.

But of course it had, which was the whole point.

Next to the photos he lay down his Army issue .45, which was already loaded, and the note that the two-lobed pumpkin had told him to write.

Are you ready, Aaron?

He turned to see the figure in black emerge from the edge of the woods behind and to his right. It looked like black smoke in the bright daylight, and stayed to the shadows at the edge of the tree line.

He knew he should be frightened — but for the first time since that moment in Somalia when he had pushed his friend away from the antipersonnel mine, he felt absolute peace and — *happiness*.

It's time, Aaron.

The black figure seemed to melt away and then reform, but its words were right next to his ear.

Aaron nodded, and bent down to pick up the .45. The pain in his leg was gone.

Go ahead, Aaron.

He turned away from the writhing black figure, and put the .45 to his head, next to where the voice was speaking to him, and looked down at Orangefield — which was suddenly surrounded by a ring of orange, as if all the pumpkins he had ever tended had sprung back to life, just for him.

He opened his mouth in delight, and made a sound of joy—

And pulled the trigger.

Chapter 18

In his white cell, Jordie heard what sounded like a distant gunshot.

It must have been very loud, to get through the inches of padding on the walls. There was no window, except the tiny round one set into the door, above the food slot, and Jordie imagined there was thick concrete behind the padding.

Weird that he could hear a gunshot.

Or anything else that wasn't in his head.

At least they'd left him his meds.

It was just about the only thing they had left him. He couldn't remember much about the last month, and they'd tried to stabilize him every which way they could — with shots, electroshock, therapy — but nothing had worked. He knew he had a silly grin on his face, but what else could you have when basically you were a blank? He was as blank, and white as the walls, which was just fine with him. Maybe if they'd given him some Scotch and weed, his head would have straightened out.

He had said that to the shrink — one of them, at least — but if he remembered correctly, it hadn't gone over very well.

But the pills — they'd left him those.

They'd tried every day to get the combination right. But so far nothing had worked. Each day at eight in the morning and six in the evening, a little tray with a different assortment — green and yellow, yellow and white, white and blue, blue and red — was shoved through the slot, while a moony face with a bald head watched him from the little round window set in the door.

And each time he'd shrugged and taken whatever pills they'd given him.

And he stayed a blank, as blank in his head as a white sheet of paper.

Here they came again — which meant it must be eight in the morning — or six at night.

He looked at the tray resting in the slot's retractable shelf and shrugged. He shuffled in his paper slippers over to the door and took the tray.

The shelf immediately retracted.

He looked for the moony face studying him, but the window was empty.

Then he heard a tinny, shrill voice behind the slot, which opened again. Now he heard the voice more clearly: "Hey nutball, it's Halloween! Happy holiday!"

He smiled and shrugged. "Whatever," he answered.

The moony face appeared in the round window, laughing at him. It was a round face for a round window, only now it wasn't bald but had bright orange hair.

Suddenly the hair was gone and the face was bald again.

The slot pushed open again. "Like my fright wig, nutball?"

The face went away.

Jordie looked at the tray on the floor.

The pills were orange and white.

A faint connection was made: *Halloween!*

Now he recalled at least that: costumes, pumpkins, cutouts taped to windows, trick-or-treat, candy.

Candy.

Candy corn — it had been his favorite.

He took the three pills — two orange, one white — from the tray and popped them into his mouth.

They didn't taste like candy corn, but they felt hard against the back of his throat, just like candy corn would.

Those pills will make you right, Jordie.

The voice.

Like a Pavlovian dog hearing its signal, Jordie immediately began to look for his list. But there were no pockets in the orange jumpsuit. He dropped to all fours and began to search the cell, looking behind the toilet, the bolted-in white sink, under the one-piece steel cot with a single sheet covering the foam mattress and the flimsy pillow. He pulled the pillow out of its lining, turning the pillowcase inside out, studying it closely.

It had to be in there, it was the only place the list could be—

No need for lists anymore, Jordie. Don't worry about it.

There it was again, the Voice. He hadn't heard it since they'd packed him off to this place after that mess at the police hearing — *"schizophrenic delusions, paranoia, violence brought on by medication imbalance, the abuse of narcotics and alcohol."*

He remembered that hearing well enough.

Do you remember what you did, Jordie?

"Not much."

Would you like to?

"I don't think so."

What do *you remember?*

He sat down cross-legged on the floor, and tossed the pillowcase aside. "I remember I stopped taking my meds. Just like you told me."

That's right. And what did you do after that?

"I did some bad stuff. That's what they tell me. But I remember a rockin' d.j. gig in there. Pumpkin Days. Best show I ever put on." He smiled, letting the beat of his music come into his head.

What about the bad stuff you did, Jordie? Do you recall any of it?

Still hearing a heavy techno *thump-thump* inside his head, he said, "No way. Don't remember any of it. But I bet my mom'll give it to me good, I ever get out of this place."

Soon you're going to remember all of it. Every second of it. The pills you took are the ones you need to stabilize you, Jordie. You'll be as normal as before you met me. I've been...shall we say, fiddling *with your medications for a couple of weeks. The various combinations made you do some very interesting things.*

"Cool," Jordie said, working his hands like they held drum sticks. "Did I do anything funny? I used to do funny things when I was a kid. Once I jumped off the roof of Josh's garage, on a dare. And not at the bottom of the roof, but at the top, where it came to a point. Broke my friggin' ankle. Rode my bike into a wall once, too. That's when they found out I needed the meds."

There's not much funny about what you've done lately, Jordie.

"Huh." A sudden clear image swirled into his head, out again. He stopped his drumming motions.

Him pushing a knife into Josh's belly, in his kitchen.

"Weird."

The music started up again in his head, and again it stopped when another image swirled in, his Aunt begging for her life in front of the fireplace in their house, on her knees in front of him covered in blood, screaming for him not to —

"Whoa." The music was gone, replaced by nightmares. He went into a fetal position on the cement floor and closed his eyes, willing the images to go away. But they were getting more and more real — him holding a blade up, licking blood from it — a sawing sound as he worked on the body in the chair — the heads lined up on the kitchen counter —

"Make it stop! Make it stop!" he gasped, pulling at his own head.

But the Voice was silent.

The images connected into scenes now, and he saw everything as it became more and more clear: what he had done to his friend Josh, what he had done to his Aunt, *what he had done to his mother* —

A long hiss of pain escaped him, but still the images became even more distinct: the bodies in the cellar, his propping them up, covered in lime, into poses, his roasting and eating his Aunt's hand —

There's only one way to make it all go away, Jordie.

They were so real now, so much a part of what he'd done, so much of what he was —

They'll discover that the meds have balanced you, Jordie. The memories will never go away again.

He opened his eyes and said in sobbing awe: "I did these things?"

Oh, yes, Jordie, you did them all. And you'll never forget. Unless you do what I say...

He quickly followed the Voice's instructions. First he left a message, gouging his wrist with his teeth until enough blood flowed to write on the wall with. Then he fashioned what he needed from strips of the single sheet on the bed. One end of the makeshift rope he secured around the faucet of the sink, and then he sat on the floor and tied the other end around his neck.

Quickly, Jordie, before they find you and make you remember forever.

He had a momentary lapse of nerve — and the remembrance of what he'd done came rushing back into his head — all of it at once, like a large-screen movie, the silence in the house, the smell and taste of blood, the bits of flesh under his fingernails —

Now, Jordie. Just fall over.

He did as he was told.

Good.

And then a miraculous thing happened. The horror movie in his head was turned off. He was on the top of Josh's roof again, at the apex, making windmill motions in the air with his arms and shouting, "Will you laugh? Will you laugh?"

The day was bright and sunny, and he felt warm air rush by his face as he jumped, shouting gleefully, hearing the whoops of disbelief and wonder from his friends, and then he hit the ground —

Chapter 19

The doorbell rang.

As Kathy Marks hurried to answer, it rang again, twice, insistent, with a murmur of voices behind it.

"Coming!" she called out.

She opened the door to another gaggle of costumed children. This group was composed of three pirates, with appropriate black buccaneer hats bearing skull and crossbones, blood-red scarves knotted around their necks and cutlasses. One of them had a plastic knife clenched in his teeth.

"Aaargh! Trick or treat!" the other two shouted.

Kathy smiled, and dipped into her black plastic cauldron filled with candy. The pirates greedily watched the booty into their bags.

"Thank you!" they cried, sounding very much like children as they bounded off her porch, making way for a mixed group of space aliens and witches behind them.

There was a lull after this bunch, and Kathy folded her arms against the chill and leaned against the open door. The night was perfect Halloween — cold and crisp, with a gibbous moon rising over the houses across the street. There were pumpkins everywhere, carved and lit, faces alive, faint breeze stirring their fires within. Every porch light was on, and some houses sported more than the usual window decorations of skeletons, broomstick-borne witches and black cats — a few were lit with orange bulbs across their gutters, and two were involved in their annual battle to outdo one another, with giant papier-mache spiders nesting in rope-made webs, and full-size monsters — Dracula on one lawn, the Mummy on his neighbor's — guarding their homes. The street was alive with marching costumed children, mostly in bunches, their adult chaperones safely warm in vehicles at the curb; there was a veritable caravan of cars, minivans and SUVs crawling up one side of the street and down the next. Distant cries of "Trick or treat!" wafted through the air like falling autumn leaves.

A perfect Halloween.

But Kathy still couldn't get Annabeth Turner off her mind.

Shivering, she closed the door and went through her neatly furnished living room into her small, tidy kitchen, punching the girl's number again on her wall phone and waiting while it rang. She was about to hang up after ten rings when a click on the other end announced that someone had picked it up.

"Hello?" Kathy said hopefully into the receiver.

"Wha..? Whoosit?"

It was Annabeth's mother, obviously drunk. "Mrs. Turner, this is Kathy Marks—"

"Tol' you stay 'way! No damn social services—"

Fearing the woman would hang up, she interrupted her: "Mrs. Turner, is Annabeth home?"

"Who? Don' know. Mus' be a dream..." As if coming to her senses, she added, "Tol' you no social—"

Kathy hung up the phone.

At that moment she decided she had to make sure the girl was all right.

She was suddenly sure that protecting Annabeth Turner was what she had been waiting for all these years.

She stood looking at the phone for a moment, something dancing at the edges of her mind, and absently rubbed at her left forearm.

Faintly impressed there, mostly hidden by years of scarring, were the words, which had been carved with an opened paper clip many years ago, an act which she didn't remember:

THREE WILL SHOW THE WAY

She threw on a coat, and filled the candy cauldron to the brim with all the candy she had bought. Leaving now, at the height of trick-or-treating, was sacrilegious, and she could expect her house to be at least egged, if not shaving-creamed or worse. But she taped a hastily written note to the front of the cauldron and set it up on a planter-stand on the porch after locking the front door. The note read: *Take Just One, Please!*

She had no doubt the candy would be gone, and quickly, when that note was ignored — but it was the best she could do.

She had some trouble getting out of her driveway — a minivan was blocking it, and the driver nowhere to be seen.

But then she appeared, dragging a wailing bat-costumed boy of about five after her, shouting, "I told you, eight o'clock! You have enough candy!"

She pushed him, still wailing, into the van and drove off.

The night was alive. Things seemed a little more frantic this year, a little more on edge, a little more electric than usual. And there was a meanness in the air that normally wasn't present. Kathy felt a prickling in her skin, as if the sky was alive with black autumn, with Halloween itself.

There were lights from pumpkins, porches and decorations everywhere along the few blocks she had to navigate to the main road. A group of teens, who seemed to be talking on a street corner, suddenly turned when she stopped at the STOP sign and, cackling, lobbed eggs at her car. Two eggs hit the passenger side window and stayed there, like yellow eyes. She swerved, cursing herself for doing so — they were only *eggs*, for heavens sake — but the look on their faces, pinched, almost angry, made her step on the gas and speed away. She heard them hoot after her, and watched them, in the rearview mirror, physically attack the car behind her as it stopped, smearing eggs over the windshield and climbing up onto its roof.

She kept a little above the speed limit after that, until she entered the Turner's neighborhood.

Things were pretty much the same here as on her own street — except for the Turner house, which was dark, unlit. Already there were long lines of shaving cream across the front windows and siding, and the mailbox was covered with broken eggs. As Kathy got out of the car she saw a little girl, dressed as a princess with tiara and gold slippers, standing in the street, crying. At her feet was a dropped sack spilling candy.

Kathy took a step toward the girl and as if out of nowhere a woman appeared, shouting, "Get away from her!"

Kathy froze as the woman grabbed the girl with one hand, scooped up the spilled bag with the other, and hustled both off down the street, leaving a small scattered pile of candy bars and tiny candy boxes behind.

Somewhere a dog howled, long and mournful.

The moon, high in the east now, yellow as squash, was occluded by scudding clouds.

Kathy walked to the Turner's front door, stepping over a broken pumpkin and an abandoned bicycle wheel.

A convertible full of teenagers roared by, shouting abuse. A line of eggs flew to Kathy's right, peppering the already vandalized house.

The front door stood wide open.

Kathy put her head into the darkened entry, and said, "Hello?"

A cat hissed and ran out past her, into the night.

From somewhere in the back of the house, beyond the stairway to the second floor, came a mournful sound, a miniature of the dog's howl she had heard.

She stepped into the house, nudging aside a lopsided pile of newspapers which blocked the hallway with her foot. The pile collapsed, papers spilling like playing cards.

The pained sound came again.

"Ohhhh."

"Mrs. Turner, it's Kathy Marks. I'm in your house."

"*Ohhhhhh.*"

Kathy slowly walked down the hallway, passing the living room, which was filled with deep shadows — furniture at odd angles, boxes that looked as if they had never been unpacked.

The sound came again from the kitchen.

Kathy stepped into the dimly lit room. There was a low-wattage bulb under the stove hood which was the only steady illumination. A round ceiling neon flashed once, stayed off. Everything looked orange. There was an open, unlit refrigerator, a door to the backyard, blocked by an open garbage can beside it, the smell of bad eggs and sour milk, a small rectangular kitchen table with a window over it peppered with filthy dishes.

On a chair pulled up to the table at an angle facing the room was the slumped figure of Mrs. Turner.

"*Ohhhhh...*"

Mrs. Turner tried to raise her head but only managed to lift it high enough to moan again. Her face was bleary with drink. She lifted her right hand slightly, trying to reach the nearly empty blue vodka bottle which teetered on the edge of the table. There was vomitus in a pool on the table and on her left arm, on which she lay her head.

"*Ohhhh, dreaming...*"

Her right hand fell against the blue bottle, knocking it off the table. It fell but didn't break, sloshing some of the remaining clear liquid on the dirty floor.

Mrs. Turner sent up a louder wail.

Kathy Marks approached. "Mrs. Turner, your daughter..."

"*Dreaming!*" Mrs. Turner screeched, throwing herself back on the chair and pointing with a wavering right hand out the window behind her. She fell partially forward, now spying the blue bottle on the ground, and pushed her chair violently back, dropping to the floor and scrambling after the remains of the vodka.

Out through the window Kathy saw unclear movement in the moonlight: a figure and something under a tree —

The librarian moved forward, around the moaning figure of Annabeth's mother, and peered out the window —

"*My God —*"

Annabeth Turner was trying to kick a chair that supported her aside. A rope suspended her by the neck from a sturdy branch of the tree —

As the librarian watched, the chair fell aside, letting the girl swing free, arms at her sides.

"*Annabeth!*" Kathy Marks screamed, moving frantically to her right. She pushed aside the garbage can which blocked the back door, knocking it over, spilling fruit peels and used slices of lime. She yanked the door open.

There were three wooden steps down to ground level. The top slat broke, sending her foot through and catching painfully at the ankle. She pulled it out, ignoring the pain.

She ran for the girl.

The moon overhead was completely covered by clouds at that moment. The night became darker and colder.

Far off she heard the beginning of a roar, and the ground began to tremble.

Dogs howled as if in unison, and every light in Orangefield, as if on cue, went out.

The night was filled with a hush, followed by an unearthly, keening cry. Overhead, the sky became impossibly dark, and a darker shape, boiling out like black ink, began to fill the heavens where stars and the moon had been.

The girl became still.

"Annabeth! No!"

Kathy Marks grabbed Annabeth by her middle and held her up. She was a dead, cold weight. The librarian tried to upright the fallen chair with her foot. Moaning with frustration, she let the girl down and quickly reached down and set the chair upright, then stood on it and took Annabeth in her arms again, lifting her against her own body while she worked at the noose, loosening it then tearing it away from Annabeth's neck.

She lowered the girl to the ground.

"Annabeth!"

The girl lay cold and still, and the librarian took her by the shoulders and shook her.

"Annabeth, please!"

The girl gave a choking gasp, and looked straight up at the librarian.

"Nothing!" she cried. "I saw nothing! He lied!"

Around them, the keening sound retreated, deeper darkness retreated, the lights in the houses around them blinked back on.

The night was filled with a sudden deathly silence.

The moon slid from behind the clouds.

Not her. You, Kathy. Finally, time to remember.

Kathy Marks gasped, looked around.

That voice. Like the voice at the library — like a voice she suddenly remembered from so long ago...

Time to finish it, this time, Kathy. Remember...

Memories, which had been locked safely away since she was eleven, began to flood back into her, a jumble of unrelated images, and she gasped again—

Don't you remember, Kathy? Remember it all now...

It all came screaming back at her, suddenly sharp and clear, as if the door to a locked room had been kicked open.

A cold Halloween, colder than she ever remembered...

She ate her cold cereal at the breakfast table with her aunt and uncle, just like always. Uncle Edward was in a sour mood this morning, some trouble at the bank — but as always when he left, after carefully folding his newspaper and leaving it next to his empty egg cup and plate of toast, his empty orange juice glass and coffee cup, he rose and pecked his wife on the cheek and kissed Kathy on the top of her head. Today he pushed something into Kathy's hand and whispered, "For Halloween. Have fun." As he was leaving, closing the front door behind him she looked down to see two crisp dollar bills, folded in half, in her hand.

Aunt Jane's hand quickly covered her own and pried the money loose. "I'll take that," she said primly, unfolding and studying the money, then making a snorting sound before putting it in the cookie jar, a fat green bear, on the shelf on the wall over the table. She gave Kathy a cold look. "Finish your cereal and get off to school. You'll understand when you're older." Then she added, "Or maybe you won't." She was staring toward the closed front door as the sound of Uncle Edward's car faded down the street. After a moment she spoke again, in a soft voice, still facing the front door. "Just because you're his kin don't make you mine. When your ma and pa died I told Edward not to take you in. I told him five times. But he didn't listen. He said your pa was his brother, and that made him beholden." Annabeth saw that her hands were trembling, and a single tear tracked her hard, pinched face. "I told him," she said, a dry, bitter sob.

School was school. At lunchtime she talked with her friend Mary for a while, then went off by herself, behind the big elm, to talk to Sammy.

"How are you today?" Sammy asked, in a particularly jolly voice.

"Fine. How are you?"

"You know I'm fine, because it's *Halloween!*"

Sammy gave a laugh, and Kathy couldn't help smiling.

"How are things at home, Kathy? Mr. Marks still being bad at night, after the lights go out?"

Kathy said nothing, and her face darkened.

"Oh, don't be cross! You know we've talked all about it. You know you can tell me anything."

"Yes..." Kathy said in a whisper; she was thinking about the two dollars in her hand that morning...

"Did you put that fun mark on your arm, the way I asked?"

"No..." Kathy said, looking at the ground.

"Why not?" Kathy knew he would be angry, but he wasn't as angry as she'd feared. There was still happiness in his voice. Still staring at the ground, she drew the large paper clip from her pocket.

"And there it is!" Sammy laughed. "Why don't we do it now — we've got time!"

For perhaps the tenth time, Kathy carefully unbent the outer section of the clip, making it straight. She poked at the point idly with her finger.

"Aw, don't worry, it won't hurt! I won't let it!"

Again he laughed.

Holding the paper clip in her right hand, she turned over her left forearm and pressed the tip into the flesh. She pushed it in harder, seeing a drop of red blood rise from the skin.

"Now just make the words!" Sammy encouraged.

"Hey, Kathy—"

Her friend Mary was suddenly standing there, eyes wide. She stared at Kathy's arm, at the paper clip.

"What are you doing?" Mary asked.

"Nothing." Kathy lowered the paper clip, hiding it in her right palm.

"Who were you talking to?"

"Nobody," Kathy answered.

Mary shook her head. "They were right about you. I was going to invite you to trick-or-treat with me later, but you're *nuts*."

Mary turned and ran off.

"Hmmm?" Sammy asked, after a moment.

Kathy drew the paper clip out again, and began to carve words into the flesh of her arm as Sammy encouraged her and laughed.

Just as Sammy had predicted, they sent her home after the nurse examined what she had done to her arm. Mrs. Marks and a beating were waiting, and then there would be no trick-or-treating.

And then Mr. Marks would come home from the bank, and night would come...

"But we don't care about any of that, do we?" Sammy said. "Because today you're going to see your ma and pa, right?"

"Yes..."

Walking down Main Street from the school toward home, Kathy noted a few strange things: an ambulance screeching through traffic toward the hospital, and then another from the opposite direction, and then, two blocks along, a crowd gathered around the front of the bank, and police cars.

"Let's go into the park!" Sammy said suddenly. It was the first time she had ever heard him sound like a grownup — almost in a hurry.

She crossed the street and entered Rainer Park. The trees near the main road were covered with toilet paper. Farther on, the park was almost empty. She passed a few mothers with babies in strollers, all of them bundled up against the cold. Some of the babies wore Halloween costumes, cat whiskers, pink angel's wings. A touch football game was just breaking up; the football, tossed errantly, came to a rolling stop at her feet and she stood looking down at it until an older boy came and scooped it up. He paused to look into Kathy's face, and at her blood-dried arm.

"Man, you're *weird*," he said and ran off, scooping up the ball.

Keep walking, Sammy said, and suddenly his voice was a bit more urgent. He had begun to talk inside her head. *You know the spot.*

Kathy was cutting diagonally across the park, toward its farthest borders. There was a grove of trees here. It was the site of picnics in the summer, with its permanently mounted barbecue grills. But once the weather chilled it became almost empty. Kathy had seen no one here the last time she had visited, the day before. There was no one now.

"Ah!" Sammy said. His voice was natural and jolly again. He seemed to be walking alongside her, though she couldn't see him.

And then she *could* see him, his black cape swirling in and out of focus, like fog, his laughing face hidden, a hint of chalk white...

"It's still here, Kathy! Just like we left it!"

She stopped before a huge oak, one branch reaching out over its own fallen leaves like a long thick arm. From it hung a perfect hangman's noose. Below it was a three-legged stool Kathy had stolen from Uncle Edward's basement bar.

"What do you say, Kathy?" Sammy laughed, but then he became very urgent indeed —

Do it.

Kathy heard a faraway noise, a group of voices growing louder — but then Sammy was filling her head with only his voice:

Do it now, Kathy. Climb onto the stool. You'll see your ma and pa. Put the rope around your neck. Just like I promised. Tighten the noose. Kick the stool away.

Away —

Kick it —

Away!

And then she was floating in air, her ears filled with a roaring sound, Sammy's laughing voice, other sounds like voices carrying across a crashing surf, she felt the faint cold breeze of her own swinging body, then something very indistinct opened in front of her and the voices all went very far away, pulled down a long tunnel away from her like chattering little mice and there before her —

"Ms. Marks!"

She was in two places at once — then and now. She was yanked back and was there, in 1981, feeling her body hoisted up and opening her eyes and choking, gagging, unable to breathe, the boy with the football gawking at her from below, a policeman, and the other men who were lifting her while another ripped the noose from her neck—

—and now, in the present, she opened her eyes and saw that she had climbed up onto Annabeth's chair, put Annabeth's rope around her neck, and kicked the chair away—

Now, Kathy.

Finish it.

Go there.

See your ma and pa.

Annabeth was standing in front of her, screaming. Then she turned and ran toward the house. There was a great commotion and noise, and then the girl reappeared, running toward the tree, a long knife in her hand.

"...Cut you down..." the librarian heard Annabeth say.

Kathy began to struggle, trying to reach up and release the pressure on her neck.

Finish it or I'll take the girl.

Annabeth stopped halfway to the tree and began to fight for breath. She collapsed, the knife falling from her grip, and began to writhe on the ground.

The caped figure materialized over her, like a black swirling cloud. For a brief moment it turned its cowl toward Kathy and she saw a horrid paste-white flat face within, black holes for eyes and a mouth in the shape of a perfect 'O', full of emptiness.

She dies unless you finish it.

The girl was fighting to draw something from her pocket, and then found it, an inhaler. It rolled from her grasping fingers onto the grass.

Do it now.

Kathy let go, and closed her eyes.

"All right," she sighed.

And then she began to lose consciousness, felt the weight on her neck squeezing, Sammy's own fingers squeezing the air from her—

"Ha ha!" Sammy laughed. "Time to finish it!"

She felt the ground begin to tremble again, heard the hush followed by a high keen, darkness enclosing the earth, the stars and moon blotted out—

"Time to see ma and pa!"

As when she was eleven, the indistinct place opened in front of her, and what had been only bright clouds began to form into something else, shapes, moving shapes—

She thought she saw—

"Ha ha ha—!"

A curtain dropped down. She fell. Air came back into her lungs, and Sammy's voice was gone, shut off in mid-laugh.

Slowly, the night came back to her. She heard the sound of a dog barking, the laughter of children, a far-off shout of "Trick or treat!" She felt the cold of the autumn night breeze on her face, and wetness of dewed grass on her fingers.

She felt sweet cold air in her lungs.

Kathy slowly opened her eyes.

Annabeth Turner knelt on the grass beside her. The inhaler was pressed tightly to her mouth. She drew a long ragged breath and then lowered the instrument and put it in her pocket.

"You—" Kathy began.

"I wouldn't let him take you," she said.

The librarian raised herself on her elbows. She saw the knife and cut rope beside her on the grass. She looked at Annabeth, who was suddenly crying.

"He promised to show me—"

"I...saw..." Kathy Marks began. "I...saw...some... *something...*"

The young girl fell into her arms, crying, and Kathy held her for a long time.

Around them, Halloween went on. The moon came out from hiding, became sharp and white and round, with a smirking face. On porches, candled pumpkins flickered bright, and, up and down streets, children dressed as monsters of a thousand kinds pounded on doors demanding candy, and filled handled bags and pillow cases to the brim with goodies. Trees rattled their bone branches, and made the wind moan through their wooden instruments. Black cats tiptoed under circling, flapping bats.

And then — a curious thing happened. Came curfew, and then midnight. The pumpkins lost their fiery faces, the monsters scattered, and the porch lights went dark and the window cutouts were hard to see. The winking Halloween lights went off, and the papier-mache spiders went to sleep in their vast rope webs.

The world went quiet.

Tomorrow it would all be gone, all of it.

Halloween was over.

Chapter 20

You have failed.

That's true. What are you going to do: kill me?

You're usually not one for levity. You must know how disappointed I am.

We've tried this twice now, and it hasn't worked. Perhaps it's time to try other things.

I agree. We have few enough opportunities. Though, as you realize, it will be more difficult.

These...creatures are fascinating in many ways. A mixture of weakness and tenacity and, sometimes, surprising strength. The girl and the woman...

You sound as if you almost developed feeling for them. They were the reason you failed.

They were too strong, ultimately too resilient.

Perhaps we should avoid females in the future.

Perhaps. But there's a toughness in many of them, regardless of gender.

Would you like to return to the time of burning wicker men, stuffed with goat innards and human criminals? Or perhaps to an earlier time still, when they crawled on all fours through their own fetid muck—

Your own levity is noted, Dark One.

They have known both of us by many names since the beginning of this wretched place. They will know me again.

I shall succeed for you yet.

And then I will rid this world of every atom of life.

Yes. I'm glad I let the girl and woman possess the merest hint...

Hint of what?

Never mind. Don't be alarmed.

For someone who's failed me, you show a remarkably cavalier attitude. It seems to me we have much work to do.

Yes. There's always next Halloween...